Rafferty

Hugh Rafferty hopes to see out his retirement in peace. The former Texas Ranger wishes to swap the days of conflict and fighting for calm on the small ranch in the remote high country he now calls home.

It seems some people have other ideas. When gunslingers repeatedly launch attacks on his ranch, Rafferty assumes these are figures from his past, out for revenge. But, as clues develop, he learns there is something much bigger afoot.

Rafferty must return to old ways if he is to outwit these men, and he must call on allies from his past to help him overthrow the bandits who are after his ranch and his life.

Rafferty

Pete Bridger

A Black Horse Western

ROBERT HALE · LONDON

© Jan W. TenBruggencate 2015
First published in Great Britain 2015

ISBN 978-0-7198-1660-4

Robert Hale Limited
Clerkenwell House
Clerkenwell Green
London EC1R 0HT

www.halebooks.com

Typeset by
Derek Doyle & Associates, Shaw Heath
Printed and bound in Great Britain by
CPI Antony Rowe, Chippenham and Eastbourne

CHAPTER ONE

They came out of the gully at a full gallop once they knew their ambush had failed. Two men, guns blazing, their horses raising a broad, low cloud of dust at the mouth of a narrow ravine.

'Gosh, boys. I wish you didn't think you needed to do this.' Hugh Rafferty spoke quietly, settling in for the fight.

Rafferty lay in hiding behind a granite outcropping. He had abandoned his coffee pot and his small, smokeless campfire with the first boom of the attackers' rifles. Now he watched the men who wanted to kill him. They rode hard and fast. They'd thought they could surprise him, but their opening shots had missed. Now, they'd had to move. The ravine was so small at its opening into the broader valley that there wasn't room for two horses side by side. It was thus an easy spot to protect, but a bad spot to be in once enemies got through, there being just that one entrance, and no back way out.

Because they had to, bad form as it was, they came out of the ravine in single file. Rafferty held his fire, though they made wonderful targets there, framed by the rocky walls on both sides.

'C'mon boys, do that smart thing. Cut down and out of here, and you'll have a chance,' Rafferty said, in a low voice the two riders could not hear over the pounding of their horses' hoofs. They were still a good 200 yards away. Even if they'd heard the advice, they wouldn't have heeded it. They were on a job, excited by the boom of their own guns and secure in the knowledge that there were two of them to Rafferty's one. They knew too little about Rafferty, or they might have reconsidered.

Their horses separated once they were free of the confining cliff walls, giving Rafferty two targets instead of one.

They bore down on him, their shots ricocheting off the rocks and kicking splinters of granite that jabbed at his skin. These were no common cowhands. They were experienced fighters, attacking as Sioux warriors might have attacked an Army troop. Their shots, fired on the run, were close to the mark.

'You boys know how to fight. Times must be bad, you going in for this kind of thing,' Rafferty said, letting the wood of his rifle stock lay cool against the stubble on his cheek.

Their first shots had come from hiding, out of the rock pile at the opening of the ravine. But they'd missed and, from that angle, once their quarry had taken cover, they had no chance of getting him. Worse, they were themselves trapped if Rafferty was able to take the fight to them. They realized too late that there was no back way out of the rough cut they'd used for cover as they waited for him to come by. These men were keen shots, and they were killers, but they lacked a sense of tactics. They were the kind of men who would be dangerous under a good leader. They were dangerous now, but they were facing Hugh Rafferty, a man accustomed to danger.

Rafferty was dead cool, the cool that gave a man a chance to review his situation and make intelligent decisions about it in times of crisis. It was the cool that made him a reputation as a Texas Ranger, and that had saved his life more times than he cared to remember. He lifted his cheek from the rifle and turned to his horse, who was alternately watching Rafferty and the onrushing, shooting horsemen.

'You just take is easy, feller. This won't take but a minute,' Rafferty told him.

He decided that the pair must have waited a long time, drygulchers expecting him to come by this location, knowing this was a favoured stopping place. There was no way they could have gotten into the ravine after he'd stopped for a midday cup of coffee and a meal of hardtack and jerky from his saddle-bags. He mentally kicked himself for letting himself fall into a pattern that attackers could use, even on his own ranch.

'You boys are lucky you've stayed alive as long as you have. It's only because I'm getting old and careless. Well, I'm still old, but times like this, I get downright un-careless, if you take my meaning,' Rafferty said, pulling the rifle back into position, cradling it, pleased in the back of his mind with how steady it lay, how much a part of him it felt.

Drygulchers, they were. Shoot a man in the back. Shoot him from hiding. Shoot him from a dark alley when the light of his match illuminated his face. It was a thing the West didn't approve of, but not everyone in the West lived by its rules. But it was a tenderfoot trick to get caught in a place that forced them to charge from the open toward a man who had good cover. They might be experienced fighters, but these men were not experienced drygulchers. Likely they'd figured Rafferty would be killed right off, and they wouldn't need to take particular care. That was a dangerous assumption for a killer to make.

Rafferty was grim. He let the sights move on target. His finger slowly, ever so slowly, hauled back. He let himself be surprised when he felt the sudden give of the trigger mechanism, the boom, the kick. The shot knocked off one man's hat. The man had ducked at the last minute, and gotten under the line of Rafferty's aim. It wasn't as if Rafferty had missed. His shot had gone precisely where he'd aimed it. Just the target had moved some, was all. Hugh Rafferty was satisfied. His rifle was shooting just fine. Now there was no question. These men would pay for their mistake.

The fighting now became rote. Like a fine chess player, Rafferty had a set series of reactions to certain situations. He already knew how he'd deal with this one. His mind moved beyond it to the reasons behind the attack. He was thinking hard. They had known he stopped at this spot regularly while working this part of his range. That meant somebody had been watching him. Who? And why hadn't Rafferty noticed? He must have gotten lazy, letting a couple of outlaws gain intelligence on him in this way. He decided right then that he'd have to go back to his old cautious ways, even on his own land.

The attacking gunmen had moved quickly after their initial shots had missed. Missing had been their first mistake. They'd gotten to their horses in under a minute, and they'd come blasting out of the opening, a fellow in red on the left and one in brown on the right. Spurring their horses. Charging full tilt across the low, dry meadow.

It was an attack meant to confuse, to strike fear. But they clearly didn't know a lot about the man they were after. They'd pay for that second mistake. It was a bigger error than the other, for this wasn't the first battle for their intended victim, nor the second, third or fourth. Hugh Rafferty wasn't particularly subject to confusion in battle. He was a veteran of cattle wars, of gunfights with desperadoes. He was hardened and single-minded. You didn't survive the kinds of fights Rafferty had been in and won, not if you got shaken by two men on horses yelling and shooting wild.

If there was one thing Rafferty was given to in battle, it was talking. He was known to keep up a non-stop, quiet conversation with himself, from the start of a fight, right to its conclusion. As a matter of habit, Rafferty didn't talk much. He was quiet, sometimes, to the point of distraction. Asked a question, he sometimes waited interminably before responding. But in battle, he was downright chatty.

He had rolled into cover after the first shot from these outlaws, but not without grabbing his rifle. A honed reflex, knowing where the rifle lay and being sure to pick it up under attack. His horse heard him say, 'Well, now,' as he rolled. The words had startled the horse nearly much as the shot. They were the first words it had heard Rafferty speak all day.

He'd been talking steadily since they fired the first round. Once he'd taken the man's hat, he felt they were close enough for serious attention.

'Gentlemen, it's party time.' He pulled his knees up under him, and rose to meet them. He fired a couple of rounds at the attacker on the left. One of the shots caught the man's boot, or part of his foot. Rafferty saw the leg jump and the man look down quickly. It would make the man wary, and maybe it would make him worry a bit.

'Still time to run. Still time to hide, boys.' Rafferty dropped behind a boulder that protected him from that man's shots, and he concentrated on the other one, whose outfit was the colour of the ground, of the dust. The clothes might have been any colour once, but in time the West turned everything to dust. This man was closer to it than he knew.

Rafferty laid the rifle easily up against his cheek once more and held it well out on the stock, ignoring the man's yells and his wild shots. A pistol shot from a galloping horse was a chancy thing, and Rafferty knew it. He stepped clear until he was in the open, in full view of the man. Slowly, he tightened his fist around the firing mechanism. Back, back came the trigger, and then concussion of the shot, the plume of fire and the stink of burnt powder. Rafferty ducked back behind the rock.

'Forgot to duck, eh? Sorry, feller.' He smiled a grim smile. The bullet had caught the man six inches below his collarbone, just above the pocket of his shirt. The attacker fell back, rolled to the side, and off the horse. His foot caught in the stirrup, and the horse veered to the side, bucking and kicking at the body. Whatever Rafferty's shot hadn't done, the horse did. One down.

'You suppose this guy still wants a hand in this game?' Rafferty said, with a glance at the horse. He stepped out from behind the protecting boulder to face the other attacker, but the man was no fool. He'd seen how Rafferty had handled his partner. Scare tactics wouldn't work against an old Ranger. And now it would be one on one. Under the circumstances, those were bad odds. The man in the red shirt quickly cut his dusty bay and headed down the wide valley and out of sight through the narrow opening, without a glance back at his partner.

'Smart boy, smart boy. I wouldn't want you for a partner, but at least you saved your own hide.' Rafferty didn't waste a shot on him. It wasn't a high percentage shot, and Hugh Rafferty was a man to make his shots count.

With the end of the shooting, his chattiness faded. He'd stopped to make coffee when the men had attacked, and now he went back to his small fire. One of the bullets had scattered the twigs he'd used as fuel, but enough had been left that his coffee had boiled. He stomped out the embers the bullet had kicked up and poured out a cup – hot, black and mean.

CHAPTER TWO

Rafferty reloaded the rifle and checked his pistol. He'd leave his horse back up in the patch of grass by the pines on the slope. The gelding deserved the break. They'd been going since sunrise. Like many a cowboy, Rafferty had a way with animals. He'd never ridden a horse to death. That was a greenhorn's trick, or that of a man on the run. If you were talking about days and weeks of travel, giving a horse a chance to rest now and then meant you got farther, faster than if you pushed the beast to its limit each day.

Now and then, Hugh Rafferty asked a lot of a horse, and he got it, because his horses had a lot left to give. He could read the animals. He felt the spring leaving their step, felt them beginning to plod. When they needed a break, if he could give it to them, they got it. And if it meant Rafferty had to walk, difficult as that was, well then, Rafferty walked.

Walking for him was cumbersome. He'd lost a piece of his foot during an Indian fight and had to stuff a spare sock into the end of his boot to fill the extra room. But he'd practised, and there was hardly a limp. He tried not to cater to his disability, and he walked whenever it seemed the thing a normal man would have done. Actually, he walked more than a lot of men in the West walked. There were men who, if it was a job that couldn't be done from the saddle, they'd refuse to do it. Rafferty was not such a man. Rafferty

11

was from the school that said if a job needed doing, you just went ahead and did it. Honest work took many forms, and as far as he was concerned, you shouldn't judge a man by the kind of work he had to do to make ends meet. You could judge him by how he treated other people, or animals, or you could take it for granted he was a good man until he proved otherwise.

There were two men who had proved otherwise, and one of them lay out there on the dusty range.

This was the second attack since Rafferty had moved into this country. Johnny Dunedin, the young gunfighter who'd once been given a break by Rafferty, came after him. It was fast and final. Dunedin pulled a gun on Rafferty, but his gun misfired on the first pull of the trigger and then his bullet ploughed into the dirt on the second. Rafferty's smooth draw brought his shooting iron up and even. He fired twice, killing the young man where he stood. Rafferty thought Dunedin's attack had been related to something out of his past, but now he wondered. These men were after more than Hugh Rafferty the man. They wanted Rafferty out of the way for some other purpose. But he couldn't figure out what that purpose could be.

Rafferty walked out into the open, the coffee cup in his left hand and the rifle in his right; finger in the trigger housing for a quick shot if it was needed. But it seemed there had been just the two of them, and the fellow in the red shirt didn't look like he'd been making for a place from which he could stage a second attack. He'd been in full flight.

The dead man's horse stood wide-eyed and heaving, his rider's body still hanging by the foot from one stirrup. Rafferty talked to the animal low and easy as he walked up, finally putting down the coffee cup. The man in dusty cloth-ing was unrecognizable from the beating the dragging and the horse's hoofs had given him. Rafferty gave a jerk on the foot, and it fell free from the stirrup, leaving the torn body in a heap. The horse reared and ran. Rafferty let it run. He searched the body, finding nothing but the man's empty holster and a bag of makings in the shirt pocket below the bullet hole. The bag seemed heavy. He opened it and pulled out a shiny twenty-dollar gold piece from among the bits of tobacco. Interesting, but still nothing that helped identify the attacker. Well, the horse would find its way home, and whoever had sent the men would get the message. It'd take better men than these to finish Hugh Rafferty.

He set down his cup and dragged the body over to the side of a rock outcropping where he tumbled stones and dirt onto the corpse. Rafferty didn't have shovel or pick with him, but any man deserved not to have his body torn apart by carrion birds. Rafferty wiped his hands on the grass and went back to his coffee cup. He stood for a moment, looking down the valley where the second man had gone.

Then it struck him. Johnny Dunedin, too, had been carrying a twenty-dollar gold piece. A nice, shiny one like this one. Coincidence?

Thinking, Rafferty walked back to his fire, poured another cup of coffee, and threw what was left in the blackened pot over the embers. He looked out over the land. This was the country he'd chosen for his home. He'd purposely picked land few others would want, specifically so he wouldn't have to fight for it. So his sons, if he ever had any, could be ranchers instead of gunmen. Rafferty himself had done enough fighting for a half-dozen generations.

It was high country he'd chosen, most of it vertical, but with good, tall grass in the floors of the valleys, where he could pasture enough cattle to keep him busy, and cut enough hay to get the animals through the cold mountain winters.

It was beautiful country, rich in pines and precipices.

Now that the echoes of the shooting were past, he could hear again the sounds that had entranced him years before, when he'd first seen the country. A low wind in the treetops; small creatures beginning to move again after their paralysis during the gunfire. The whiskey-jacks, which some folks called 'meat hawks', returning to their high-sided nests in the pines and scolding from the high branches. The mountain chickadees whistling brightly. The satisfied neigh of his horse on the rich grass above him.

It was beautiful country, but now somebody was after him again. And that put it in a new light.

Was it the past or the present that had launched this attack?

Was it Rafferty himself they wanted, or his land? Or was it something else, he wondered. If something else, what could that be? Rafferty wasn't a man to sit and wait. He decided to take it to them; give them something to think about.

The question returned. What might it be? There used to be Indians on this range. He found their arrowheads now and then, and the blinds they built of stone, overlooking trails used by the game they hunted. High up on the cliffs of jagged canyons he'd found drawings in the stone; drawings so high, they'd have had to have used ladders to make them.

There was history in this land, and because human beings, no matter what their culture, tended to look for the same sorts of things, he'd found a sign of the older inhabitants. At one of Rafferty's own favourite camping spots overlooking a green glade he'd found pieces of pottery that indicated that earlier humans had liked the spot, too. It wasn't the kind of stuff made by the Indians in these parts now, but something from an older people.

Folks found a place, stayed for a while, and then left or were driven off. People were people, regardless of colour or

tribe. It should be no surprise that the peoples of different
centuries, of different ages, would like the same kinds of
places. A place that provided good shelter, game, water and
a fair amount of security was a good spot for anybody to
find. It wouldn't be surprising if someone else might have
liked the RS Connected range just for that. But Rafferty
knew it was more than that. If someone was willing to kill for
the place, it was more than just the love of the land. There
was one thing behind it: money. He didn't have an idea yet
how someone figured to profit from this land enough to
justify paying fighting wages, but he meant to find out.

Rafferty sat and thought until the horse nickered, telling
him it was time to move on. He was loaded and astride in a
minute.

He took a roundabout route into the nearby town, and it
took him almost three hours. He rode past the settlement
called Springwater and entered from the side opposite the
direction from which he'd come. No point in making it too
easy for them. At the saloon, he draped his reins over the
rail out front, checked his pistol, and walked in through the
swinging doors.

Rafferty didn't have many friends in this town. Fact was,
he didn't really have any. He'd spoken to a few of the townspeople, and he'd done business in the general store. He'd
been seen at the saloon on occasion, cutting the dust from
his throat, but he wasn't a mixer, and most of the townsfolk
weren't his kind of people. In a sense, they were the future,
the ones who'd build towns into cities, centres of com-
merce. Rafferty was of the past; a man of the wide range, a
wanderer. But he was changing with age, settling down.
That linked him to the people of the ramshackle old struc-
tures and the increasingly neat new ones that formed what
they called a town.

Hell, they were even talking about changing the name.
Springwater, the argument went, wasn't a proper name for

a town with a future. But nobody could agree on what other name to use. It had been Springwater for the fifteen years since old man Carruthers had parked his wagon here, noted there was water nearby and that a few trees grew on the hillside, and decided to stay. Springwater was the nickname for the brook that was started out of a spring on the hillside, ran less than a mile, and then disappeared into the sand.

The town had had a rough beginning, gambling and gunfights and all the other vices that spiced the life of many an early town in these parts, but it was changing. A couple of folks were trying to grow some crops, and a schoolmarm had been hired to give lessons to the children of townspeople and ranchers in the area. They hadn't gotten as far as a schoolhouse yet. The teacher was an elderly woman widowed by a gunfight in which her husband had been a mite slow. She had come from an East Coast family and was educated. In this rough country, where most got their learning from the land, she would ride from ranch to ranch, tutoring and leaving lessons to be prepared in her absence. It wasn't much in the way of education, but it was more than many settlements had. Most of the ranchers had no formal education themselves, but they wanted it for their offspring, and were willing to scrimp in other areas to provide for their children.

Rafferty wasn't quite one of their kind. Not yet. He was still one of the wilder ones. One of the old school, you might say. And he rode into town for one of the old reasons. For Rafferty, there was just one place in town he'd find the kind of men he was looking for, and that was the saloon. He ordered a whiskey and turned his back to the bar to study the occupants of the place.

Just a scattering. A couple of cowboys at a table by the door, and three men at a table in a dark corner by the street-side wall. Over in the corner, where the bar met the unpainted plank wall, sat a drunk. He was talking to himself – or to the room at large, it wasn't clear which – but he was talking.

'I moved out of Texas finally. That state is getting entirely too civilized. Somebody counted a few years back and figured out they had nearly 820,000 people in the state. Hell, there's four or five times as many cattle as that. But, hell, a cow never seems to take up as much of your space as a person does. I've felt all alone with a thousand head, when I've felt hemmed-in by just one or two folks.'

Rafferty took a minute to let his eyes grow accustomed to the darkness. The three men at the dark table didn't look right. Not cowboys, not dusty enough. These men didn't spend their days following the herds. Rafferty noted the way their guns hung in well-worn holsters, the polish of one man's boots.

The drunk kept talking.

'Yep, that and bob wire. They've started fencing parts of Texas. Days of the free range down there are done for, as I see it. The big, pow'ful ranchers, they're spending the money to fence out the squatters, the sheep-herders and them. Some of those nesters, they figured it works both ways; they do a little of their own fencing, to keep everybody else out. Everybody cutting each other's fences. Everybody shooting at everybody else. But the way it looks to me, they're not fencing the others out. They're fencing their ownselves in!'

Just the way the men at the saloon table looked suggested to Rafferty that they were gunmen. Maybe outlaws, maybe lawmen, maybe men who worked for fighting wages. One with his back to the wall had turned, and all three of them were watching him as closely as he was inspecting them. He figured it was as good a time as any. He picked up the glass and held it out.

'I'm drinking to the man who bought this drink,' he said

in a voice that carried easily throughout the barroom. The heads turned his way. One of the men at the corner table piped up.

'Man ain't got no friends. Drinkin' to hisself. Ain't it a shame.'

Rafferty smiled, pleased to have gotten a response. It made the continuing easier. He turned to the speaker.

'You are mistaken, my friend. The man that bought this drink isn't here. Not in this town. Not in this world. The man who bought this drink is wolf meat just now. The vultures have him open at the gut and they're having a fine time with him, hauling his innards this way and that. Not that he didn't deserve it. He came after the wrong man. Tried to drygulch Rafferty. Failed. But he had a twenty-dollar gold piece in his pocket, and he left that to me.'

'How do we know you didn't drygulch this feller?'

'A witness. The man's partner, who turned tail and ran, his red shirt flapping in the wind as he abandoned his associate. Left the man there to die. Never stopped to check on him.'

'Red shirt? Why that'd be Jack, Jack Henry. He never ran from nothin'.'

'Jack Henry got a touch of lead in the leg, or maybe just his boot or stirrup. He was scared, and he ran. That is the truth,' Rafferty said.

'You're lyin', mister,' the man said. If the bar was quiet before, it now took on the sound of a funeral home. No one made any extraneous noises, nor made any unneeded movements.

The speaker got up and took three steps toward Rafferty. He stood with a hand hovering over his pistol butt, leaning slightly forward, feet spread. In the west, you didn't call a man a liar without being prepared to support your claim with lead. Rafferty lost no composure.

'If he hadn't run, he'd be dead too, and I'd have two

twenty-dollar gold pieces to spend. As it is, he can take his to Mexico and spend it. Anywhere he likes, as long as it isn't here. Because if he's seen around here again, he'll be dead.'

'You talk mighty fine for an old man,' the man said. Rafferty looked him over. Not much more than a boy. A punk. Maybe eighteen years old and long ago gone bad. He had the look of a young man with physical gifts, good coordination, good speed, but who'd spent the proceeds from the use of his talents in too many bars. His eyes were bad, too. Rafferty, for all his experience, was not yet forty, and in as good shape as he'd ever been in. He was cool.

'Rafferty'll kill the man in the red shirt, and he'll kill every penny-ante gunfighter that comes after him. It's going to take more than a twenty-dollar killer. . . .'

Rafferty had gone into his fighting babble. The words came out of some other part of his brain. His attention was sharp and focused. He had been watching the young man, and watching the group behind him. The others were looking on with interest, but did not seem to be threatening. The boy, on the other hand, was on the verge of drawing his gun. Rafferty had been talking big, letting the boy get madder. And now, that little light of madness came to his eye, that little light that telegraphs that someone is going to do something he shouldn't, and the boy's hand went for the gun.

Rafferty stepped in quickly. As the boy's gun came out of the holster, Rafferty swept down with a left hand, hitting the wrist. The pistol went off with a boom that filled the room. With his right, Rafferty grabbed the boy's greasy hair and pulled his head down, hard, against a raised knee. He felt the crunch of a breaking nose. He took a firmer grasp on the gun hand, breaking the firearm free, and swinging the arm behind the kid's back. The boy twisted and bent partially over backward. Rafferty snapped a knee into his kidneys, pulling the arm ever tighter. He gave it one more jerk, and there was a pop as the boy's shoulder dislocated. Rafferty dropped the body. A bloody face, a busted arm, bruised kidneys and a reputation forever ruined in this town, the boy fell in a heap at his feet, sobbing. The whole thing had taken just seconds.

Rafferty stepped backwards to the bar, dipped down to pick up the boy's gun and scanned the scene to be sure no others came forward. None did. He put the gun on the bar, picked up his drink and finished it.

'You tell the man who sent you, boy, not to send punks and not to send tinhorn gunmen. If he wants Mama Rafferty's boy Hugh, he'd better come himself or leave well enough alone.

'On the other hand, those twenty-dollar gold pieces come in handy. If he wants to get shed of a few more, Rafferty will be waiting up there in the hills. But send good men. Send men with sand. The ones I see around here are hardly worth Rafferty's time. He'd just send me or one of the other hands out. The RS Connected has plenty of time for it, being as we don't have too many cows up on the range just yet. Won't have much to do for a while. Plenty of time for fighting.'

The bartender spoke quietly, ignoring the blubbery moans of the boy on the floor.

'You mean you aren't Rafferty?'

'Me? Well, I guess I look like him, some. But you get him riled, and Rafferty's twice the man I am. I mean, Rafferty's mean. And he's spooky. He's about as spooky a feller as I've ever come across. I hear tell when he was a Ranger, riding the outlaw trail, he had his personal flock of vultures, followed him around. If he was trailing you, you could always tell how close Rafferty was by the black birds, hovering high over him, knowing where he went, there'd be dead meat, human or otherwise. If I was one of these boys, I can tell

20

you, I wouldn't want to be tangling with Rafferty. Not him. No, sir!'

And he walked out, shading his eyes against the brightness of the sun after the dark bar. He didn't want to stay too long, to give the others time to think about the fact that they outnumbered him in a small space. So he stepped right out into the sunny afternoon. As he went, he heard one of the men from the corner table speak.

'Nobody said he had hands up there. Simon said Rafferty was supposed to be alone.'

The subject of the statement smiled and climbed on his horse, heading quickly out of town before they got enough sense to follow him.

The drunk, who'd stopped to watch the fight, picked up where he'd left off.

'Another thing. I think horses are gonna disappear in Texas pretty soon. No reason to climb on one, they got so many railroads abuildin'. And they're busy writing laws. That's what you gotta do when folks ain't got room to turn around and spit. You need laws. Wrote themselves a constitution this year, I heard.'

That was the last Rafferty could hear. He was out of town in a minute or two. He rode so as to leave an indistinct trail, but not too indistinct. If they sent more men after him, it would give him the opportunity of making his point more forcefully.

CHAPTER THREE

He realized fairly quickly that he wasn't alone on the trail. He had a pretty good lead, but somebody had followed him. He picked up their dust a way out of town. He waited until he was around the bend and out of sight. Then he turned his horse a sharp left and began working up a sharp rise, right up the side of it. The horse was a mountain-bred mustang and went easily, head bobbing as it picked its footfalls, the muscles on the big hindquarters rolling.

Rafferty selected his spot carefully. He knew this country. He'd covered it enough times, and used the experience of a former Ranger to keep his mind sharp. He knew all the ambush spots, the hideout spots, the places to lose a trail and the ones where a lost trail could be picked up. He cut off the trail on a rocky section where he'd leave no sign. He got up over the rise and dismounted. Spoke quietly to the mustang and left it standing.

Two men walked their horses along his path. They weren't coming fast. Clearly they were simply tracking his route, not chasing him at this point. Perhaps they'd be looking for likely ambush spots along the path. They wouldn't know that Rafferty seldom used the same trail twice. That was how he had gotten to know the country so well and that was why the riders would find no easy, hoof-worn route to follow.

Rafferty smiled. He'd have a little fun with these boys. He'd been thinking up tactics ever since he'd seen their dust. Now he was ready.

Rafferty put his hands to his mouth and began a low, unearthly howl. It was enough like a wolf's call to be mistaken for one at a distance. He started softly, and made successive howls louder and louder, just until one of the men stopped to listen. Rafferty could hear their voices.

'Hey, did you hear that?' one said on reining in.

'Hear what?'

'Well, I don't know. Like a wolf. Some kind of moan or something. Soft, like it was far away.'

'You're hearing things, Clancy.'

'Yeah, maybe,' the first man said. They rode on, but they'd been lax in looking at the trail, because until now, Rafferty hadn't been trying to hide it. Now they began looking again, but they'd already gone past where he'd turned off. Rafferty got on his horse and rode back down the hillside.

He came up behind the two, pulling his rifle from the scabbard and laying it across his pommel.

'You boys looking for me?'

Both riders jerked their horses around and faced him. He had the drop of them, and they weren't tinhorns. They wouldn't try anything.

'No sir, just ridin',' said the man who'd heard the howl. A cautious man.

'This trail don't take you any place you'd want to go. This is a bad trail to be on, actually. Strange things happen on this trail, even way back to the early days. The Indians didn't even use this trail. Bad medicine. You boys, well, maybe you want to just head back where you came from. This country ain't healthy for people who don't know it real well.'

'How's that?' asked the second rider.

'Yeah, what do ya mean?' added the first.

'Well, Clancy,' Rafferty began, having heard the other use the name. 'Well, I guess it's a lot of things. Like I said, this here is strange country – strange country to be sure. People say the local Indians used to call it sacred ground. Yeah, and I've seen some old Indian sign hereabouts. Seen what look like old ruins in some caves, and other such. Don't look like they're from any tribe I've ever heard of, but they're not from white men either. Nothing like you ever seen.

'What I hear, I guess the recent Indians hereabouts were a little scared by it. They have a legend about a ghost wolf pack. You can hear them, sometimes, the wolves. I've heard strange things growling outside the cabin sometimes late at night. I don't figure they're ghosts, but then I never went outside to check, either. And they're supposed to attack people who camp out in the open, I hear. Me, once I heard that, I always made sure my camp was protected.

'We're not scared of any old tribe legends.'

'Fine with me. Everybody learns their own way. But right now, I'm asking you gents real nice to turn around and head back the way you came. This is nigh onto RS Connected range. It's not on the way to anything else. Somebody might get the wrong idea about what your intentions were.'

The man who'd heard Rafferty's wolf-call got the hint, and turned to go around Rafferty's horse and head back.

'Let's go, Slim,' he said, giving Rafferty the other man's name. But his partner wasn't going quite that easy.

'Hold up, Clance,' he said. Clancy stopped right next to Rafferty. The move put men in two different quadrants. Rafferty couldn't cover them both with the rifle. He had to move before they recognized their advantage. Rafferty made a low clucking sound. The mustang's ears perked and the horse backed up a full length. Rafferty now had both men in front of him again.

24

'You and Clancy need more pushing, Slim, you go ahead and balk.' In an instant, his pistol was in his fist, pointing at Clancy's chest, and he'd worked the mustang just a bit, so that the rifle was now pointed at Slim's chest.

'Now, I want you to know this. I try to be a peace-loving man. I don't like killing men, but I haven't got as old as I am getting pushed around.' Slim got the hint.

'I'm not bracing you, mister. Just talking.'

'Do your talking and be on your way.'

'It's just that, well, we heard there's gold up in that country. Heard Rafferty pays his bills down at the store in gold, and in dust and nuggets, not gold money. Well, we was just thinkin' we'd take a look.'

'Do I look like an honest man, Slim? Do I look like a man whose word you can trust?' It occurred to Slim that what Rafferty looked was downright mean, but he just kept on talking. 'I am an honest man. Believe me. There's nothing in that RS Connected country that you'd be interested in. Nothing at all.

'You tell the man who gave you that information he'd better come up to the RS and get the story straight before he spreads any more lies. You tell Simon that. Now get on your way.'

The men went by him, and Rafferty backed the horse in a circle, keeping the pair in his gunsights. He'd heard the name 'Simon' in the bar, and it was a calculated risk to try it on these fellows. They hadn't looked questioning, so he figured it was a name they knew. Trouble was, he didn't know any Simons, first name or last. He'd have to keep his ears open. Meanwhile, there were these two fellows to deal with. He followed them a short distance to make sure they kept going, and then he cut back to the side, using a rough old trail that let him cut their path a mile away. From a hidden spot, he watched them go by. And once they were well past, so they couldn't spot him, he loosed a long, loud howl. This time both men heard it, turned in their saddles to look back and then headed out at a gallop.

CHAPTER FOUR

Rafferty got his horse and headed back into the high country. It would be dark when he got there. All this shooting and fighting took up a lot of time. A cattleman working his range alone couldn't afford too much of that.

He took a circuitous trail back, cutting up over a ridge. He rested his horse at the summit of the ridge, pulling up under a big old tree to make himself less visible on the horizon of anyone who might be looking. He checked his back trail. The valley below was small and dry, but opened into a larger one with a stream. After an hour, he let his horse drink while he chewed on some jerked beef. When the cabin came into view it was in moonlight. Rafferty pulled up and scanned the countryside until he spotted the figure of his big dog, Wolf, loping across the meadow toward him in the night. When the dog arrived, he spoke a word to reassure him, and they trotted to the cabin together.

Rafferty got some meat for the dog. He pulled his gear from his horse, watered and brushed the animal, and turned it loose into the tall grass. Then he crawled into his bed, exhausted. He slept a dreamless sleep until suddenly he dreamed he'd been shot in the arm.

The big dog had dropped his considerable snout on Rafferty's arm. When Rafferty hadn't woken, the dog had

27

lifted his head and dropped his snout once more. That made Rafferty start from sleep, clawing for his gun until he recognized his surroundings. He looked up. He'd latched the door and locked the dog inside.

'Sorry, fellow. You'd think a man didn't trust you to give him fair warning, locking the place up that way,' he said to the dog, his weathered hand working around the dog's ears, scratching and massaging. The dog's eyes went to half-staff, his snout rose and one leg thumped the ground in reaction to the attention. Finally Rafferty got up, stretched, and opened the door. Wolf loped out the door and up toward the trees. After finishing his business, he would make a broad loop around the property, sniffing out anything out of place, chasing a rabbit or two, pointing at a couple of birds. That was his morning custom.

Rafferty gathered kindling, used some shavings to get his fire started, and fed it wood until there was enough for coffee. As it caught, he filled the blackened pot from the water bucket he brought in whenever he came by the well. As the water heated, he dumped in a few spoons of coffee, adding eggshells to settle the grounds.

He sipped a steaming cup of his coffee as the frying pan heated and he added a few more sticks to the fire. Rafferty sliced bacon into the pan and, when it started to sizzle, he quickly mixed up biscuit dough in a cracked bowl. He added water, got a nice mixture going, and moved to the fire. He turned the bacon, pushed it to the side of the pan and dropped in two gobs of dough. More coffee, and he lifted the crispy bacon to a plate, dropped in three more spoonfuls of dough. A minute or so later, he took his coffee and a plate of bacon and biscuits outside to eat them sitting on one of several stumps out front. The stumps passed for chairs, sawhorses, exercise weights, and in winter, firewood. He ate slowly, watching Wolf on his rounds. When the dog finally returned, Rafferty let him finish off his plate before he washed it out.

A little log smokehouse squatted up against the slope near the house. Rafferty had several cuts of meat curing in the well-built structure. He'd built it firmly both to keep the smoke in and to keep animals out. He went over and cut a chunk of meat for Wolf, who'd failed to bring home a catch from his morning rounds.

Rafferty picked out a dun from his remuda, saddled it and headed up into the back country of the ranch. He had no specific goal, but such reconnoitering rides inevitably ended in some kind of work. It was a way of keeping track of what was happening on the range. Such a ranch was the RS Connected that there didn't need to be a lot of make-work: he had few fences, so there was little fence-mending to be done; and the cattle didn't tend to roam out of his range. At some point he'd want to isolate some of his stock from others, but it would take fairly short stretches of wire across the mouths of canyons to accomplish that.

Rafferty enjoyed such rides, too, because they challenged his old tracking skills. He couldn't hope to see every creature that had crossed the ranch on a single ride, but he could pick out the sign of many of them, and learn something about them.

He was well into the day when he found the carcasses of three of his cows in a fairly small bunch of narrow canyons at the back of his ranch's confused system of valleys, gulches and washes. Two were quite old, but the evidence was clear. They had not died of natural causes: they'd been killed. He found the marks on the white cattle bones of the teeth of a predator, probably a cat of some kind. The third carcass was newer, and the remains of the meat showed the predation clearly. Rafferty got down and inspected the kill. A killer cat on a cattle ranch needed to be dealt with, and it wouldn't do to let the situation continue while he fought off his enemies, or he might not have a ranch left to come back to when the fighting was done.

Close scrutiny of the evidence confirmed for him that the cow had indeed been killed, and while vultures and other carrion eaters had been there, it was a cat that had done the killing. The recent kill confirmed the suspicions he'd had from looking at the other two piles of bones.

A good-sized cat, and one that had no compulsion about taking cattle.

Some cats kept to the wildest country, lurking around the game trails, and feeding on wild animals. They were not much of a problem for a cattleman. Indeed, they tended to keep the wild game stocks in good health by weeding out the older and weaker animals. For a high country rancher like Rafferty, that was important, as a fair part of his food came from hunting the game with which he shared parts of the ranch.

But a cat that had learned to take cattle, and did it repeatedly, was dangerous. Cats could kill and kill, taking more meat than they needed for food. The first two cattle carcasses Rafferty had found had been roughly equally old and not far apart. It suggested the cat hadn't killed both for food.

And it meant Rafferty would have to go after the predator.

He considered the situation. He'd have no luck trying to backtrack the cat from the most recent kill. Cats were very difficult to trail in any case, and a track days-old would be virtually impossible to locate. He needed something else, and it seemed to him the cat would have to come down to water; like most other animals, cats went regularly to waterholes. He went over his mental map of this part of the range. The most likely spot was the little lake a couple of valleys over.

He headed out. The dun picked its way expertly between the rocks when Rafferty left established trails. They took a route that rose out of the dry sections over the valley bottoms and gradually up toward the piney woods that surrounded the lake. Rafferty pulled the horse to a stop at the crest and looked down.

It wasn't much of a lake; more of an oversized waterhole in size. But this was chill mountain water. A patch of water a hundred yards long and not quite as wide, shaped like a bean, a sort of oval with one concave side and another convex. A wall of rock dropped as a cliff into the water on the one side, while a fairly steep, pine-covered slope ran down the other.

He guided the horse down.

This was a good spot for hunting, and the game trails formed a mesh among the pine needles, guiding the animals down to the water by dozens of different routes.

The water was clear and had a blue tint at midday. Rafferty had caught fish here, but now he came on the hunt for the cat and to water his horse. He followed a slanting path, ducking occasionally to miss being slapped by a pine bough. The trail had been established by deer, not riders, so it was clear only about as high as a man on foot.

When he reached the shore, he stepped off the horse and let it drink. Years as a tracker accustomed him to be constantly on the lookout for things out of place. That was what tracking was all about. When tracking a man, it might be a cracked branch, or a bit of clothing caught on a thorn, a fireplace, or the butt of a cigarette. With animals, there was less to find, but signs remained. Trails, paw and hoof-prints, bits of fur, the remains of meals. They all gave information to the skilled tracker. More than one of the old mountain men had instructed Rafferty, and his skills after many years matched the best of them. He walked a short distance down the shoreline, inspecting the tracks of game that had come down to the lakeside to drink. The sign of the cat stood out. A big one, something new for this area.

Rafferty picked out the pads of its feet, immediately distinguishing it from the tracks of his big dog, Wolf, by the retracted claws.

It was unlikely there would be two cats this big in the area, and the size of the pads matched his estimations of the size of the predator.

Rafferty crouched by the sign, comparing the fringes of the tracks with features of surrounding tracks. He knew from observation when certain animals tended to water, and it helped him determine the age of the tracks. He knew little about this cat, and he was forced to determine its most recent visit by the age of the other tracks around its own. The rough, pebbly sand made the work difficult, but it was clear to Rafferty the puma had been here recently. Very recently.

He looked up at the horse. It knew. The animal had finished drinking, and now it had caught a scent. Likely it was that of the cat. The dun was alert, nervous, and it stamped uncomfortably. Rafferty jogged back to the horse, speaking in a low voice. He wanted his hands on the reins before the horse's self-preservation instincts told it to bolt. The dun shied as he approached, but he made a dive and caught the trailing reins. Rafferty stood by its neck, peering into the woods. The horse had caught the smell of the cat from upwind. Rafferty scanned the area, first the nearest line of trees and then focusing deeper. The horse grew more anxious. Now its eyes were rolling. The cat was near.

It might not have caught the smell of them because of the direction of the wind, but by now the cat would have heard the horse. Rafferty began leading the mount along the lake's shore, away from the source of its displeasure. He could spot nothing in the woods. A cat most likely would stay away from them, but it was not wise to take too much for granted about mountain lions, and particularly about one that had taken to attacking cattle.

He wondered whether the cat might have been wounded, since a sick cat might go after easier prey like lone cattle. But there was no sign of an injury in its tracks, and the cows the cat had taken appeared to have been healthy ones. A healthy cow is a skittish animal and can be a dangerous one. Rafferty climbed into the saddle and headed up away from the lake, taking a route as far as possible from where he suspected the cat was. His trail took him by an outcropping rock face, and as he approached, he studied the rock. A cat sometimes took position on a ledge over a game trail, dropping from overhead to the backs of unsuspecting prey.

Rafferty had to make a judgment call. The horse's attention when it caught the scent appeared to have been directed at an area in the woods to Rafferty's left. The cliff was to the right. The cat could have moved, or the horse could have been reacting to something else. Rafferty pulled to the right, along the cliff, and kept his attention to the forested area to the left. He saw nothing at first, but when the trail passed closest to the rock, he glanced up just to see the beast on a ledge bunching for its leap.

His pistol leapt into his fist and fired at the blur of tan. A second shot from the big weapon diverted the cat's leap only slightly. Rafferty spurred his horse in time with the second shot. He ducked down onto the horse's neck. The puma flew past, landing in a heap on the forest floor. The smell of the cat drove the dun into a panicky uphill gallop. Rafferty fought to keep control. He heard in the midst of it a man's voice.

CHAPTER FIVE

'This way, boys. He's down this way.'

There was nobody who'd be after him for any healthy reason, so Rafferty let the horse run for a while, giving it its head. The dun ducked and swerved between the trees, finally cresting the hill overlooking the lake. Rafferty guided it onto a trail he knew, and slowed it slightly. The horse was beginning to labour as the excitement wore off, and if men were after him, Rafferty would need the animal's strength.

A mile farther, he pulled back to a trot to let the horse catch its breath.

He looked back, but could see nothing along his back trail. Perhaps the quick run had misled them?

The three men on the trail had located the site of the cat attack, and had dismounted to study the animal's body.

'Must of come from up on the ledge there,' said one.

'If it did, he must have had plenty of notice. Couldn't ask for a pair of nicer shots. One through the neck into the heart and one through the mouth. Damn cat was dead when she hit the ground. Probably never even scratched him.'

'He didn't have notice. If he'd seen that cat ahead of time, he'd have taken another route. This Rafferty can shoot. They told me he was good, but nobody said he was this good.'

'Yeah, but there's three of us and we taken money to do him. Let's go to work.'

The adrenalin was worked off and the run had taken its toll of the dun. They slowed to a walk. The horse was lathered. It was nearly an hour later when Rafferty caught sight of the three riders, just a quarter mile behind. Two broke into a gallop at the sight of him. A third held still long enough to loose a rifle shot that smashed a rock five yards from him. Rafferty knew the dun couldn't handle a hard chase yet. He looked furiously for a place to fort up. Pistol rounds were in the air, but the men had little chance of hitting him from horseback and at this distance. If Rafferty's horse could last, there was a spot half a mile up ahead where the trail swung around a big boulder. If he could keep a lead until then, he could hold them off from the spot. He leaned forward, talking to the horse, and when its stride seemed to falter, he urged it with a rocking of his body to a regular gait. It was pulling its head, straining at the reins when he rounded the boulder at full tilt and dropped off the horse's side. The dun, freed of the burden of a demanding rider, came to a stop, its head down and sides heaving.

Rafferty had pulled his rifle loose as he dropped, a manoeuvre he'd perfected in the Rangers, and one specifically designed for escape from a horse shot out from under you in a fight.

He rolled against the side of the boulder.

The three came around the rock in single file, still at full speed. Rafferty took the first one out of his saddle with a single shot. The second and third reined in at the sight of Rafferty's standing horse, then wheeled around at the sound of the shot that felled their leader. The second rider had his pistol out in a flash. It fired into the ground as Rafferty's rifle's slug caught his neck and drove him backwards off his mount.

The third man quickly raised his arms in surrender. Rafferty had the killing in his blood. He set down the rifle and held his hand out to the side, inches from his holstered pistol.

'This is an even break, mister. More than you were giving me. Take it!'

The man's eyes opened, and he took the chance. He was fast. His hand grabbed iron and brought the barrel up. A triumphant, ugly grin found itself on his face. He had beaten Rafferty to the draw! He fired, missed, and took Rafferty's more considered shot in the shirt pocket. The man fell as limp as the puma, and as dead.

Rafferty walked among them. Only the second man was still alive, and he had little time left.

'Who sent you?' Rafferty asked him, kneeling by his side.

The man coughed, turning his head away. Rafferty asked again. The voice came out in a croak.

'Simon,' he said.

Rafferty pulled the man up by the shoulders to make him more comfortable, but the man was already dead.

The ranger went through the pockets of the three men, and made a pile of what he found.

There was a likely looking collection of soft rock near the upper edge of the big boulder. Rafferty got up and used one of their own horses to drag the bodies one by one to the side of the boulder. Then he got up above it and broke free a small shelf of stones. They rolled down over the bodies. He took a few more and dropped them over the corpses to completely cover them.

He took the bits of paraphernalia he'd collected from the three and packed it in the saddle-bags of one of their horses. He took out a small notebook and wrote the description of the place, explaining that the men had been killed and where they were buried.

Rafferty led the horses to a camping spot some distance

away, letting his horse rest while he made coffee. Late in the afternoon, he pulled up outside the town of Springwater. He loosed the three horses and watched them trot into town.

Rafferty turned and made his way back to the RS Connected.

CHAPTER SIX

Far away south and west from Rafferty's ranch, Jim Dunedin was mining gold.

He'd found himself a likely spot, panning a small stream and following the colour up the water until he was able to locate its source. Not a vein, but a rich talus under a steep hill. He was building his waterway, having gone upstream to a spot with enough elevation, staked out the channel, and begun digging.

The soil was such that he could simply dig a ditch for part of the distance, saving the cost and effort of hauling lumber and constructing a wooden structure.

He was a watchful man. A worker, but one who took regular breaks. With each break, he would move his rifle from where he'd last set it down to closer at hand. He would scan the surroundings, slowly, having memorized the land-scape and searching out any changes that might indicate someone's presence.

It was on one such break, the shovel stuck into the dirt and his rifle in a huge fist, that he caught sight of the rider working his way down the narrow trail to Jim's camp.

Dunedin casually pulled out his right-hand pistol and checked the loads. They were, of course, ready for action. By now he'd recognized the man as George Sample, a friendly miner who had a little money but had had no luck finding gold. He'd offered Dunedin a fair amount for his claim, but Dunedin hadn't been interested. He was probably here with another offer, Dunedin figured. He wasted time checking the rifle's action, and finally the man was there.

'Got some bad news, Jim. The stage driver told me what was in it. I guess whoever sent it told whoever he sent it with, and the story come down the line along with the letter,' Sample said.

'Well, I don't need no story. Give me the letter.'

He carefully opened the dirty envelope with his sodbuster. As he read the letter, the big man's shoulders seemed to drop. Finally, he folded it and slipped it into the pocket of his shirt.

'I'm sorry, Jim,' Sample said.

'Yeah. You still want this claim, George?'

'You going? I wouldn't want to take advantage of your situation. I knowed your brother being killed and all, you might have to go.'

Dunedin nodded.

'Ain't gonna be no taking advantage. I'll sell this claim to you right now for the price you offered me last month. It was a fair price then, and it's fair now. Take it or leave it. If you don't want it, I can get the same price or better from someone in town.'

'It's a deal, Jim. I'll buy the claim. I know you might have got a sight more if you'd had time. I shore do thank you.'

'That's fine, George. I'll know it's in good hands. There's some folk around here I'd as soon didn't have my claim. I'll throw in all the tools around here. I'll only be taking my travelling gear and my horse. Everything else is yours. Let's head into town and get the paperwork out of the way.'

'That's it, then? You're taking out?'

'Something I got to do, George.'

Dunedin pulled his guns out of the holsters and held

them out to a wide-eyed George Sample. There was no malice in his gesture.

'I'll be picking up a new set of pistols in town. You interested in these?'

'Why, they're like new, Jim. Why'd you want to give them away?'

'George, these I ain't giving. These you'll have to buy. I heard Shuck Tyler at the Emporium talking about having some new Peacemakers in. Figure to pick up a matched pair. I like a new gun.'

They settled on a price, and Sample went and caught Big Jim's horse while Dunedin collected a few things from his stained, dusty tent. He packed efficiently. In minutes, the man had wrapped up a few belongings in a blanket, tied them off with piggin' stings and then bundled everything inside his long, black cloth coat. Outside of Jim's few tips on the mining of the claim, there was no more talking.

By the end of the day, Big Jim Dunedin wore twin Peacemaker Colts and was riding east.

CHAPTER SEVEN

Rafferty rode with a watchful eye as he came to the cabin that was his ranch headquarters.

If there was to be a war, there was much to do. Rafferty was a man alone, and he had range and cattle for which he was responsible. His dog – that huge, hairy creature of indistinct origin – pranced out as normal to greet him a half mile from the cabin. He said a few words, and the dog took place alongside the horse, accompanying them into the yard. Rafferty fed the big dog with the meaty end of an antelope thigh. It would keep the animal busy for a day or two.

Rafferty had a suspicion this dog was actually part wolf. He'd found the animal near a waterhole at the edge of the desert. At the time it was just a pup, and had been sucking off a bitch mastiff that had died within a day of Rafferty's arrival on the scene. Later, he learned the bitch had most likely belonged to a member of British royalty who'd come to America for hunting, but whose party had been broken up in Indian battles a year earlier. The pup's mother had apparently been on her own since then. From the sign, it looked to Rafferty as if she'd fought off a big cat. The cat had carried off the rest of the litter, but the old dog had been able to save one. The bitch was badly hurt, and had been unable to hunt after the attack. The pup had continued to suckle its dying mother, but had also begun to hunt.

41

It managed to catch a couple of field mice. The pup was thin, but wiry. It didn't want to leave its mother, but finally followed Rafferty after he'd buried her. They'd been friends since, with Wolf taking up the role of sidekick, watching while Rafferty slept and guarding the cabin. Sometimes the dog trotted along on rides across the ranch land, but more often he ranged around the cabin area when Rafferty was on the trail. Wolf knew to get water from one of the waterholes Rafferty had built around the place and was actually fully capable of bringing down small game for his food, but Rafferty fed him regularly to keep the dog from having to roam too far. Today, having given the dog the antelope leg, Rafferty switched horses and picked up his gear, leaving Wolf to look after the cabin.

He was three miles away when he made his sleeping place, a spot with grass for the horse, with a commanding view, and with a way for retreat. It was a place, like several he had identified on his ranch, where he could rest in comparative safety. He was unlikely to be seen, protected by a small rock outcropping. He could look down on the common approaches, and few wise men would risk the exposure of those approaches. And, on top of it all, he had a good horse, who would be as good as the dog at warning him of danger. The horse was resting easily, and Rafferty slept that light but refreshing sleep of the outdoorsman.

He built a small fire before the dawn, lighting tinder from the dry material under a pine, twigs and needles bleached light grey. He selected materials, as he did whenever it was possible, that were entirely dry and would make little smoke. These were the fires he made regularly in the country, smokeless fires built without a second thought. These were the skills he'd learned in a lifetime, a lifetime of survival against the odds.

Rafferty found a comfortable spot that looked down on the valley in the breaking dawn. The coffee warmed his calloused hands, and his nostrils flared with the smell of it.

There was somebody after his ranch. That part was clear. If it had been someone after him for some personal reason, he'd have had warning. Whatever enemies Rafferty had made over the years were men, not cowards to hire their killings. The enemies of Hugh Rafferty would want him dead by their own hands.

Besides, he didn't know anybody named Simon. It could be somebody going by an alias, but that didn't change the facts before him. His enemies would want him themselves. Old outlaws would want the satisfaction of having killed him on their own. Revenge would not be served simply by knowing he had been killed. Besides, the old outlaws seldom had the money to pay for their killing.

Still, whether they were old enemies or not, if they wanted something else, if Rafferty's death was just a means to another end, they might go about it this way. If they didn't simply want the satisfaction of having killed Hugh Rafferty, then they might choose not to face him. If they wanted something else, and Rafferty was just an obstacle rather than the primary goal, they might want him softened up first. The boys they'd sent thus far had been comparative amateurs. Maybe they figured that with a little pressure, Rafferty would walk away. If so, they didn't know Hugh Rafferty.

No, this was something new, something not out of Rafferty's past. Unless, of course, he was missing something. There was always that possibility, that your best guess was wrong. In this situation, it looked like they wanted the ranch, pure and simple. Or something on it.

The question was, why? Why did they want the RS Connected?

Rafferty got up to pour himself another cup of coffee and returned to his spot, watching his horse work its way up toward the campsite. There was a spring here, and the horse would come to drink. The spot was safe, and Rafferty could wait. Besides, there was thinking to do.

The ranch was good enough, but it wasn't one that would make anyone a lot of money. The big spreads wanted wide, flat ranges, with good water and good grass in ample quantities. The RS was a maze of small, grassed valleys and gullies. It would hold quite a few head, but it wasn't an easy ranch to work and it was distant from transportation. It would be tough to round the cattle up for a drive. It was too cold in winter.

It was a beautiful place. Its glades and its waterfalls were things to behold. They were the things that had first caught Rafferty's attention. Only afterwards had he begun to look at the economic potential of the place. It had potential, to be sure, but any cattleman would recognize its limitations. It took a man of dedication to want a place like this. Rafferty was such a man. Few others were.

So, why did they want him off the land?

The man, Slim, had mentioned gold. There was talk in town about the fact Rafferty sometimes paid his bills in gold. That could have gotten around. And it was a short step from there to a rumour that there was gold on the RS. Men would do much for gold. If they believed there was enough of it, powerful men might spend money to hire gunfighters.

Maybe that was it. But it didn't make much sense. It was unlikely someone would pay money to get a ranch for its gold without hard proof there was a healthy source of the precious metal. And Rafferty knew there was no hard proof. Nobody knew this land better than he did. He was sure of that.

Or was he?

Rafferty had known of the area for years, and he'd known at once this was the place on which one day he would settle. Over the years, when he happened through this part of the country, he would stop and explore another part of the range. He'd selected the cabin site, and identified campsites through the back country. He'd picked the best valleys for summer range. High places where the cows would eat alongside the wild grazing animals. In the fall, he would bring them down out of the chilling heights to the lower pastures for wintering. These were the places he could still reach after the winter snows fell, where he could break out the hay he'd cut for when the snow was too deep, and cows could no longer get to the grass.

That was the kind of work Hugh Rafferty was doing and was willing to do for his own place. But it was work a man would have difficulty finding a cowhand for. This ranch wanted men who got down off their horses and worked with their backs. It wanted men who cut hay by hand, who stacked it and who stayed long enough to dig it out of the snow and distribute it. Few men who worked for wages did that kind of work. Riding a fence line was easier. Riding for fighting wages was easier still, but riskier. There was a difference between the hired gun and the owner. One rode for the brand, and the payday it represented. The other rode for the land itself, for what it meant to him.

Rafferty had grown to know the land, and with more knowledge came more respect. It was a place that made sense to him. There was the winter land and the land for summer. There were the springs where streams did not run. Upwellings surrounded by a patch of deep green, or wet places along a shelf on the canyon wall, glinting in the morning sun.

There was a sense in Rafferty of a history here. No one had ever talked to him of the place, but there were signs. There were mountain paths that had once been cleared, and which required only minor maintenance. There were caves whose walls carried signs drawn in clay and charcoal, signs of ancient visitation. There were campsites generations old.

And now and then, when he had cause to dig into the soil, he found layers of charcoal and ash indicating fires that were even older. The people of old, he found, chose many of the same campsites and shelters that he picked.

What did that tell him? Well, there were others who had known this land well. That meant there could be others today who knew things about the RS Connected terrain that Rafferty might not.

The horse had reached the spring. Rafferty got up and threw a loop on the animal. He walked it over to his campsite. He had a lot of ideas, but he still didn't have enough information. He could go search for more, but he still didn't know where to look. That was no problem. It was clear enough someone wanted something up here. And wanted it enough to try again. Rafferty could go looking, but it seemed clear the men with the answers would come to him soon enough. All Rafferty would have to do was wait.

In the meantime, there was work to do to prepare for the coming fights. He wanted to get some of the better animals up into the higher land. If a fight came, he wouldn't have time to be watching the herd. He wanted them settled in pastures they wouldn't leave. And he wanted them in positions that made them seem like too much work for rustlers.

Rafferty clucked to the horse, and it walked over. He threw an arm over its neck, and with it, slipped the bridle in place. He dropped the reins on a branch. The horse would hold its position there. He went for the blanket and saddle.

He heard the shot after it hit. At first, it seemed someone had clubbed him. He went down and rolled, coming up behind the saddle and taking quick stock. There was nobody there. He touched his head, and the blood was just beginning to flow. It was in his hair, above the ear. He worked out his position when it hit, and from that, determined roughly it had come from down the hill and over to the downstream side. The shot had been fired just as he

46

began to crouch to pick up the saddle. The gunman most likely had been aiming for a body shot from a long distance. Shooting up or downhill was tricky work in any case, but had he been standing, it would have been a good shot. Because Rafferty had dropped so quickly, there was chance the gunman thought it had been a successful shot. Rafferty stayed down.

They couldn't see him from where they were. He was on a little flat place, and the rocks he'd selected as protection for his campsite protected him now. It was a question of time. They'd either come after him or leave him, but as long as they were there and he was here, he was safe. The spring was nearby, and his saddle-bags were here with some food in them.

They'd wait a bit to decide how to respond to the shot. He rolled over and pulled his coffee pot off the fire. Might as well drink it while it was hot. He figured to be here a while. He took a sip out of the pot.

The shot had come from well down below. That meant he had better cover now than he would once they started moving up. He decided to fill his canteen now. He'd poured the water for coffee from the canteen rather than going the short distance to the spring. Now he crawled to his saddle, got his canteen and went to the spring.

It was more of a seep, really. The moisture dripped out of a part of the rock outcropping that protected him. It trickled down a few inches and collected in a small pool a couple of feet around. The pool would have evaporated quickly, but it was in the shade most of the day. Tracks around it indicated it was frequented by area wildlife, and this was the waterhole his horse had returned to. The horse had taken off with the first shot. Rafferty didn't yet dare look over the edge of the shelf to determine whether it was still in sight. He set the canteen up against the trickle and let the water begin to fill the canteen. He tried to get a glimpse of the side of his head in the still water of the pool, but there wasn't enough light.

There appeared to be no concussion. Just a flesh wound, although any head wound was dangerous. He pulled off his neckerchief, washed it out in the cool water and wrapped it around his head, putting slight pressure on the wound. It felt like the bullet had gone on by. Sometimes they'd get under the skin, and you'd have to track the path and cut the slug out. With the bandana in place, he would be able to wear his hat, but it would ride high.

Between two sections of the protecting rock outcropping was a crack. From below, it would be inconspicuous. There was only more rock and earth behind it. Rafferty selected that as the spot from which to make his first survey.

He sneaked out his pistol, held it up by his chin as he crawled up to the crack. Then holding it aside, he slipped his head sideways into position, looking down the slope with just one eye. Nothing. Just what he'd expected. Nobody would come right up the exposed slope. He took another angle and slowly swept the countryside. Nothing in sight but his horse, grazing and working its way back up towards him. If they waited, he'd wait.

Time. Rafferty had lots of it. He continued to lay low, moving as little as possible. He cleaned his pistol, and made sure the rifle was in good shape. He checked the loads in both. He chuckled. There were few times he'd been in a bad spot when the spot had been as comfortable as this. If they kept him here through the day, there was even some shade over by the spring. He ate some jerky and finished the coffee, which by now was cold.

He jolted with the arrival of his horse. The beast snorted and jerked at the smell of his blood. He spoke lowly, and it calmed down. That's when Rafferty realized he'd been a fool. Nobody would come up that slope. Any self-respecting killer, having taken that shot, would have left. There was no percentage in staying. If he was dead, then it was done. If not, the risk of going after him was too great. The dry-gulcher would have to hope the shot worked and leave, because if Rafferty had survived and the gunman or men waited, he'd be coming down with the setting of the sun. This was Rafferty's range. He knew it better than they.

The man who'd shot him had to be gone. It made no sense to suppose otherwise. Just in case, Rafferty saddled the horse from the uphill side, and walked alongside the horse, staying on the far side until he had a full view of the ambush site. He closed in on it slowly, and inspected the spot. One man. No cigarette butts. His horse had been tied back down the valley. Rafferty tracked him, taking most of the afternoon. The man had waited near the cabin and stayed well back, relying on his own tracking skills rather than sight to keep Rafferty's trail. The man was good.

Who was he? The head man, this Simon, or yet another of his hired guns?

Rafferty lost the trail well off the RS Connected range, where it joined one of the well-travelled trails heading for Springwater. He felt a little dizzy, shook his head and felt a jolt of pain. He recognized the head wound was weakening him. He needed some rest and wanted to check back in at the cabin. He swung the reins and crossed back onto his own range.

As he approached the cabin, Rafferty pulled up. Smoke was rising from the chimney. He cursed. Someone was there, when nobody was supposed to be there.

It had been a long day and a long ride. Rafferty had been shot and he was tired. He'd looked forward to a good night's rest, letting his horses and his big dog keep watch. The horses were all good ones, and nothing came near without their noticing. It was why Rafferty kept a corral near the cabin. Also, it provided the horses with some shelter. Both the cabin and the corral fell under a huge overhang of cliff. It saved Rafferty the cost of a barn.

But it did no good to have alert horses and a watchdog if you weren't going to be there to hear their alarm. Somebody had gotten by his defences in his absence.

He cursed again. All this shooting and killing was growing tiresome.

CHAPTER EIGHT

The town was fairly bustling as the stage rolled in. As many folks were in sight as you were ever likely to see in Springwater. That was the way it was at stage time. Folks just kind of took their business outdoors so they wouldn't miss anything.

A couple of old timers sat in chairs out front of the saloon, chatting and smoking. A litter of pale yellow slivers of wood grew before them as they whittled. One of the men just whittled a stick down, as if to make it disappear. He was a veteran whittler and carried extra sticks in his rear pocket. When one was pared down so far he couldn't easily hold it, he tossed it into the street and pulled out another. But it wasn't as if he went through sticks like water. He placed the blade with the consideration of a sculptor, sometimes lifting it and placing it again time after time. Then, with his latest slice well thought out, the razor edge would bite, his grip would harden, and another slice of wood would fall to the ground in front of the narrow boardwalk.

The other man used his worn sodbuster to carve shapes. When he finished one, he'd give it to anybody likely to accept it. The carvings were little dogs, and sometimes a horse up on its hind legs, occasionally a shapely woman.

'Here, Bill. Keep you warm nights,' he said, tossing a newly-completed female figure to a passing cowboy. The

51

cowpoke thanked him and admired it as he sauntered across the way toward the general store. The old timer spat on a stone and gave the sodbuster a few licks to restore its edge. Then he set to working on another of the chunks of wood he kept in the saddle-bags by his chair.

Over by the corral at the edge of town, a boy brushed a grulla mare tied to a hitching post. He worked extra hard at the tail, and it was tough work, because the grey horse would let loose a fierce kick every now and then. The boy held the tail out to the side, out of range of the hoofs. Nearby, the part-time blacksmith, who had a small ranch out of town, was making nails for a bigger rancher, who wanted to build an addition to his house. The ringing of his hammer on the anvil clanged through town like a bell. The leather of the blacksmith's apron was blackened with moisture at his chest. Partly, this was sweat, but much of it came from the ladles of water he poured over his face every few minutes while working near his forge.

A small group of men wandered out of the saloon, none of them particularly steady. One of the men, a talking drunk, was carrying on a conversation with nobody in particular on the history of the countryside, something that had started with an off-hand remark in the saloon about there being more people around lately.

'This country is bigger than the people that try to control it,' he said with a broad sweep of his arm out toward the open country beyond the town borders. 'It's been claimed by one government after another, but nobody's really owned it. Hell, it was Spanish, then French, then Spanish again and then British, all before 1800.' The drunk was oblivious to the fact that the others were ignoring him. He simply followed along, chatting with plenty of gesticulation.

'The United States bought part of it in 1803 and didn't know what to do with it. Parts of the place have been in the Louisiana District and the Louisiana Territory, the Missouri

Territory and in Indian Country. Then parts were in Oregon Country. And you can't leave Mexico out of it. They only signed off the territory in the Guadalupe Hidalgo treaty in '48. It's been Dakota, Nebraska, Utah, Idaho and then Dakota Territory again. Finally, in '68, they made Wyoming its own territory. Been the same for eight years now. Well, if you looked at the history, it'd be time for another change, I'd say.'

Nobody paid the drunk any attention, and he only stopped because when he paused for a breath, he realized his glass was empty. He found himself entirely across the dusty road from the saloon, and his throat was dry. As the other men watched for the stage, he staggered back across the main street of the town of Springwater and went inside for a refill.

Things slowed down generally when the weekly stage arrived. It wasn't just the activity of the team of horses and the new faces. People looked up and waited to see if someone disembarked. Springwater wasn't much more than a water stop. There wasn't a proper restaurant, and the stage went another fifteen miles before changing horses and giving the passengers a meal break. But here, as was the case across the West, the activities of the stage coaches were some of the most important entertainment to be found. A horse breeder could check out the quality of the stock, since the stages needed the best of horseflesh. A banker got word from other financial centres. The town got mail. Anybody interested got the latest gossip from the driver, any likely passengers, and the guard, if the stage happened to be carrying a strongbox. So on any stage day, the town's activities quietly gravitated toward the place where the coach stopped. On most stage days, the town slowed its pace to get the most out of the brief layover. But today, the town stopped cold.

For one thing, there was a black man riding up with the

driver. That wasn't so strange of itself. There were many
blacks in the western lands, but still not so many that you'd
see one every day. So the sight of one riding with the stage
made people curious. There were no black men in the
immediate area served by the town of Springwater, so not
only was this man out of the ordinary, he was also a stranger.
That made the town pause briefly. Then, as the dust-
covered stage settled itself at the stop and was finishing its
rocking, came the next surprise. The stage door opened
and out swung a woman – or was she a girl? Slim and pert,
with well-shined delicate boots and a chequered dress, she
had hair that was short and blonde and eyes that were blue.
They had a faraway look, those eyes did. They took in the
town in a glance, and then looked to the hills beyond, as if
there was nothing in the town of interest to her. She was a
good judge of towns. It was clear she was getting off the
stage here, and that in itself was an event. The men fronting
the saloon had been leaning their chairs back. Now they
dropped their chairs down on all fours and stared. So did
everybody else, from the cowboy with his little wooden
woman figure to the boy currying the grulla.

The black man, whose features were distinctly Indian,
dropped from the stage, landing lightly on both feet. He
pulled down a long satchel and a pair of heavy saddle-bags.
The girl turned to him. Clearly they were hers. She already
carried a heavy bag over her shoulder, but she took these
other bags from the man.

The town lotharios were caught short. Nobody had
expected a pretty woman to get off the stage in Springwater,
and they weren't ready for it. Now this black man, who'd
come in with the stage, had beaten them to the grabbing of
her gear. One of the cowboys who'd come out of the saloon
made a big deal of taking off his hat with a flourish whenever
the farmer and ranchers' wives came into town. He considered himself a real ladies' man. He was distinguishable from

the other cowboys mainly because he'd actually taken off his vest to beat the dust from it. So while the others with vests wore them with the natural pattern of dust collection, his had streaks and cleaner spots to indicate he'd knocked it against the side of a building. The black man getting the bags right away had stolen his thunder. He gave way to his frustration by spitting nonchalantly into the street.

'I'll be glad to carry them wherever you'd like, miss,' the black man said.

'Thank you, sir, but I can handle them,' she said. The cowboy with the streaked vest, accustomed to rejection, smiled to see someone else getting told off. 'I carried them to the stage, and I can carry them from it. Now, if you'll excuse me, I have to go arrange for a horse.' There was no nonsense in her tone of voice, and the man relinquished the bags. She tossed them over a shoulder and began to turn away.

The town was like the stage in some play. All activity had ceased but for these two in the street. The cowboys, the whittlers, the saloonkeeper at the door, the people peeking through windows. They were all motionless, so the rustle of their clothing wouldn't make them miss a single word. There was only the woman and the black man, and the little dust devils picked up in the street by the midday wind.

'You going riding? You know these parts, miss?' the black man said. He was impressed, given how feminine she looked, at how easily she handled the weight of her bags. He was also impressed because, having hefted the long satchel, he knew it carried at least two rifles. He'd already determined she carried a pistol in the bag she'd kept with her. This girl-woman was no one to take lightly.

'I've got to find Hugh Rafferty. I know he's in these parts, and I have a rough idea where to find him, but he doesn't know I'm coming, so I have to arrange my own transportation,' she said.

'Well, miss, I'd be obliged if you'd let me come with you.'

'I don't require any help.'

'You can be sure I know that, miss.' He lowered his voice so it wouldn't carry through the listening town. 'I know what you're carrying in your bags, and I know it's enough artillery to start a small war. I'd like to come along because I'm looking for Rafferty myself, but I don't know how to find him. And since I don't know as everybody in town should know it, I don't want to ask.'

She looked at the black man with suspicion. He saw it, and spoke quickly in a conspiratorial whisper that caused three or four residents to actually step forward in the street, as innocently as they could, better to hear.

'Be assured, miss, I'm friendly. But I hear Rafferty's a little short of friends these days. He's helped me out of more than one situation, and I'm here to stand by his side.'

'How do you know Hugh Rafferty?' she asked, having lowered her own voice as she noticed the great deal of attention she and the black man were attracting in the town.

'We fought together, in a couple of places. Mostly in Texas.'

'Did you by any chance know a ranger named Briggs?'

'Jim Briggs, well, yes. I know Jim Briggs.'

She turned abruptly and began carrying her bags toward the corral. The black man followed. She stopped, and there was a gleam in her eye, like a tear that hadn't quite formed enough to fall.

'You don't know Jim Briggs, you knew him. He was killed a month ago. A fall from a horse.'

'That's hard to believe. Briggs could stick to a horse better'n anything I've ever seen.'

'That's him. Trouble was, he was shot, and he had a little trouble holding on to the horse with two bullets in him.'

She was curt, and continued with her heavy load toward the

corral. The black man stepped back and pulled a saddle and gear from the stage.

'I guess I'll drop off here,' he said to the driver. 'My horse'll appreciate not eating any more of that dust.'

'You been good comp'ny. See you again,' the driver said. He waited until the black man had untied his horse from the back of the stage, and yelled at his team. A snap of a whip between the lead horses, and the stage led a cloud of dust out of Springwater.

The girl had made a fast deal with the blacksmith and was leading a grulla out of the corral, the same horse the boy had been currying. The big Swede in his leather apron grinned at the black man, shaking his head.

'She rented a saddle, and asked if she could have her pick of the horses in the corral. Damned if she didn't pick the best horse of the lot. I warned her that horse can be mean, but she wanted it. Knows horseflesh, that one.'

The girl stepped into the shed to change while the black man saddled both their horses. He loaded her saddle-bags on the grulla, but left her long bag with the rifles. Heads turned when she stepped out in a chequered shirt of the same pattern her dress had carried, and a pair of men's trousers. Her dainty boots now somehow looked like a good pair of riding boots. She tied the long satchel across the front of the saddle, and slung her other bag from the saddle horn.

She stood by the grulla and carefully scanned the town. The corner of her eye caught a movement in a second-floor window over the saloon. She didn't move her head, but kept her eyes on the spot. Someone had been watching from there. Watching her in secret. True, the rest of the town was looking, too, but their interest was clearly curiosity. And they kept looking. The man behind the curtain – she assumed it was a man – had stepped back and let the curtain close when she'd looked in that direction. What did he have to hide? Well, she didn't have time to find out. She was up and cantering out of Springwater with nearly every eye following her. When she came alongside the saloon, she shot a glance up, in time to see a patch of grey sleeve pulling the curtain back into place, nothing more. She went on, relaxing as she left the weathered wooden buildings.

The black man watered his horse before leaving town. He had no doubts about his ability to follow her trail. He was an accomplished tracker. Some of his detractors attributed this skill to the Comanche blood he'd gotten from his mother's side, but in fact it came from experience and training in the company of white men – men like Jim Briggs and Hugh Rafferty, both men of vast experience as cowhands, rangers, soldiers and mountain men. They were men who'd accepted him as a man, never joking about his colour, only judging him on his actions. There were few enough of such men, and for Quanah Baker, there was no limit to what he would do for them. He'd been wandering from ranch to ranch, doing odd jobs and handling cattle, when he'd caught wind of Rafferty's impending trouble. He immediately set out to join the man who'd saved his life more than once. But he'd known only the general area, and had taken the stage, figuring it was a sure way to catch the latest gossip and a good way to meet people who would know the area. The girl had been a godsend.

She would be Jim Briggs' daughter, there was no question about that. She had those same clear, blue eyes, and she had her father's thin mouth. They'd been holed up in a cave one time when the rangers were out after a marauding Sioux party. A thunderstorm had filled every gully, and Briggs, Baker, Rafferty and two others had taken refuge. Over the fire, protected by a stand of pines and the overhanging rock from the raging storm, they'd talked.

Briggs had talked about his young daughter, the light of his life, back on his little homestead with his wife and her mother. The mother had later died, and Baker had heard the wife had caught a fatal fever. Briggs had gone home to his young daughter, a girl he'd taught all the things he would have taught a son. He'd bragged, as they sat by the fire in that cave, that she could outshoot him on a still target. The men around the fire had nodded. They were all veterans, and while they were good shots in any situation, they all knew that still targets were different things from moving ones, and entirely different from targets that shot back. If you had nerve and could keep cool, you could beat a fast gun or a good shot. Fast guns weren't always accurate. Good shots fired off-target when rushed.

The men around the fire had survived because they were pretty fast, and pretty good shots, and very cool.

CHAPTER NINE

Baker caught up to the girl five miles out of town. He raised an eyebrow to see a difference. She now wore a pistol in an old holster on her right hip. The long bag was packed away behind the saddle, and twin rifles hung in soft leather scabbards from loops over the saddle horn. The bag she'd carried with her was now tied down over the saddle-bags, lighter by the weight of the pistol and holster.

She slowed to let him come up even with her, and let him have the first word.

'You look ready, Louise,' Baker said.

She started, but then smiled.

'So, you *did* know my father. And you must be Quanah Baker. He spoke about you. He spoke highly.'

'I'm flattered, and more pleased than you can know to hear that,' he said.

They rode in silence for a half mile or so before she spoke up again.

'I've wondered, and I never got around to asking my father. Are you any relation to Quanah Parker?'

'I get asked that now and then. We have different backgrounds, but more similarities, maybe. Our names mean the same thing: 'bed of flowers'. And we're both half and half. He's Comanche and white. I'm Comanche and black.

'Our trails have crossed more than once, and we keep

our distance. Quanah is a leader. You've heard of the Battle of Adobe Walls a couple of years back, and the rest? He is a determined man, and he knows what he wants. Me, I'm mostly a loner. I don't consider myself a Comanche, or a black man. Just a man. I judge others by their deeds and by how they judge me. Jim Briggs and Rafferty treated me as their equal. That's all I ask, and it's better than I've gotten most places. It ties me to them.'

He'd been watching a thin plume of dust off to the east, always a little behind, but now moving up even with them. He glanced over at it now, and she noticed his concern.

'I've been watching it, too. Just one or two riders, staying out of sight but keeping even with us. At first I thought it was you, but then I saw your dust, and realized we were being followed.'

'We did too much talking within hearing range when we were at the stage. There were people who heard us talking about Rafferty, and in a town like Springwater, it wouldn't take five minutes for our every word to be spread to everybody who was interested,' he said.

'Any suggestions?'

'You as good with those guns as your daddy used to say you were?'

'Good enough to kill the men who shot him.'

'Well, perhaps we should see what those fellows want.'

'Daddy always said it was courteous, if folks came looking, to take it to 'em.'

They went on until they had some cover, then doubled back and rode across a low ridge until they cut the trail. They rode wide, Baker to the left and Louise Briggs to the right. They came up to the two men, and weren't seen until it was too late.

The men had gotten suspicious, apparently, when they'd lost track of the two. They'd gotten off their horses below a rise, and had climbed up to try to spot them. They'd had to go about a hundred yards from the horses. Baker cut over to Louise and left his pony with her. He used his best stalking techniques to come up on the tied horses without alarming them. He untied them and walked them away. They were a quarter-mile from the two men before the men thought to look back, and by then it was an accomplished fact. One of the men yelled. Quanah gave each of the horses a slap on the hindquarters and then fired a pistol shot. Most likely, the horses would run a mile or so, then head on home, wherever that was. The two men had a six or seven mile walk back to Springwater. Baker jogged to where Louise Briggs waited with his horse, and they struck north for the Rafferty place, laughing.

'You're a pretty good Comanche, Mister Baker!' Louise said.

'Call me Baker. Everybody else does.'

'Only if you'll call me Briggs.'

'It's a deal. Now, how is it you know how to find this place?'

'I don't exactly. But Rafferty told my dad about it four or five years ago, before he moved in here. He talked about the area, and where he'd wanted to build his place. He had it all planned out. I just hope the descriptions were good, and that he built where he said he would.'

'I remember Rafferty talking about the place he wanted to retire. Never paid much attention to it. It was the kind of talk everybody came up with in the bunkhouse, or out on the range at night. But I can see what he would have seen in this country. It's like a maze, but around every corner, there's something that looks good. A lot of patches of nice grass. You couldn't run a very big operation up here, but one or two men could do pretty good work, using the box canyons and valleys to control the cattle for you.'

'Or women. No reason a woman couldn't do it,' she said.

'The way your father said you could shoot, you won't find

62

me arguing with you,' he said.

'Up here somewhere, there should be a major fork in the valley. We'll want to head left,' she said.

They came up on the cabin, finding it protected by Rafferty's huge dog. Baker got down and called to the beast, it cocked its head to listen but stood its ground, a low growl in its throat.

'Come on, boy. Come on, Wolf. It's me, Quanah. You remember me.' Baker clapped his hands low before him. He took a step toward the dog, but the dog took a step back, careful to keep an eye on both Louise, who stayed on her horse, and on Baker.

Baker talked a while, getting nowhere. It was a standoff. Finally, a light dawned. He gave a low, warbling whistle. Wolf's head jerked, and then the big dog trotted up like a pet lamb. Baker dropped to his knees, bringing him to head level with the dog, and let it shove its forehead into his shoulder as he rubbed its neck.

Louise smiled.

'I see you two have met,' she said.

'Sure enough. We're old friends. Come on down and get introduced. Then we can make some coffee and think about figuring out where Rafferty's gone.'

CHAPTER TEN

Rafferty had gotten a look into the house from three directions, working up in ways only he knew. The horses stayed quiet, but Wolf, who was inside, tipped them off. The dog gave a low sound of recognition, something between a rumble and a satisfied sigh, and walked to the door.

'Dammit, Rafferty,' said Baker, loud enough for the man outside to hear. 'You gonna keep playing around out there, or come in and say howdy? Ain't nobody in here but Quanah and Jim Briggs's girl, the one he said could shoot.'

Rafferty stepped to the front door, and heard Wolf's low greeting growl from the other side. He opened it, and the big dog gave him a snort of recognition before leaping out into the darkness.

'How did you get by that dog? Nobody's ever been able to get near this cabin with Wolf around.'

Baker spoke first.

'You forget that dog and I are old pals, Rafferty. We knew each other when it was just a pup, and the dog's got a good memory. It just took some recollection.'

Louise Briggs stood grinning, with a hand out to be shaken.

'About an hour of recollection, I'd say. I don't think that dog recognized you at all. Hi, Hugh Rafferty. You remember me, don't you.'

'I remember a runt kid with a hot pistol. That you?'

'Same kid. Pistol fits in my hand a little better now that I'm grown.'

'I imagine it does,' Rafferty said. Louise Briggs was a fine-looking young woman, even in trousers and with a holstered gun hanging from a hip.

He accepted a cup of coffee and a plate of stew.

'First time anybody else ever cooked for me in my own place here,' he said.

'First time? About time,' Louise said.

There were just two chairs for the table, but Rafferty quickly rolled up a log round and used it for a stool. He took an appreciative pair of spoons full of stew and a gulp of the steaming coffee.

'So, what're you two doing here?' he said.

'I figured I should come see Hugh Rafferty's retirement home. Dad got shot. Shows I didn't do much of a job taking care of him, I guess. Thought I'd see if I could do a better job for you,' she said.

'Somebody finally got Jim Briggs?' Rafferty stared down into the plate in a sombre silence. 'Well, I guess they'll get all of us sooner or later. The boys that shot him need going after?'

'Guess not. Guess I took care of that myself. It was a family matter,' she said.

'I understand that. How about you, Quanah? You here for the cure?'

'No, Hugh. I'm here on a family matter of my own. You're the closest thing to family I got. From what she says I guess that goes for Briggs, too. Anyhow, I was in the region when I heard you needed somebody to look after your cows while you took care of a little problem,' Baker said.

'What problem's that?'

'Word around the region is that somebody wants you dead.'

The two newcomers stood and looked at him waiting for some sort of explanation as he stood there with a blood-stained bandana on his head.

'Well, yeah,' Rafferty said. 'I haven't figured out why, but I kind of noticed that recently. At least, the evidence points to that kind of a conclusion.'

'You want one of us look at that?' Louise Briggs asked.

'Later. Let's talk a bit first.'

They talked well into the night, and were back at it before dawn. Catching up and trying to make sense of the attacks on Rafferty.

Rafferty went to a plank next to the fireplace. The plank was loose and he pulled it out.

'As good as a closet, and a little harder to find,' he said. He pulled out a rolled-up piece of paper and brought it to the primitive table where the three of them sat in the candlelight just before dawn.

'Here, let me light the lantern,' Rafferty said. 'Mostly I use candles at night, unless I'm reading and need the light. Hard to get the fuel up here for the lamp. These candles, though, I make them myself. I find wild beehives, smoke them out to get the honey, and then use the wax for candles. Beeswax candles work fine for most things.'

Rafferty found himself unusually talkative with these two. As Baker had said, they were as close as he had to family, and there'd been plenty going on he'd have liked to have talked over with someone.

They'd left the questions and answers until now. The day had been long for all three of them and, after having eaten and talked generally about where they'd been and what they'd been doing, they slept. Rafferty gave his bunk to the Briggs girl. There were two other places that passed as sleeping spots: a long workbench next to the fireplace and a wide shelf. He'd used the workbench, but Quanah Baker insisted on sleeping outside.

'Never much got used to waking up and not being able to see a storm coming. Besides, Wolf might like a little comp'ny,' he'd said.

All three were Westerners, and the bacon was frying and coffee boiling before the sun even considered giving some colour to the sky.

The paper Rafferty had gotten out was a hand-drawn chart. Rafferty held three edges down with their coffee cups, and used his pistol for the fourth corner.

'It's not much in the way of art, but it's the best I can do. This is a map of the range I claim hereabouts. Where it's nice and dark, what you see is what you get. But where the lines are lighter, I haven't been yet, or haven't been in daylight. There are enough little gullies and washes up here to keep a man busy for a long time. I been trying to get to know the better areas, and to keep track of where the cows like to go. I've got most of that, but there's still some exploring to do on this range. As I get into a new area, I come back and darken it in. It then becomes "known territory".

'And that's what I'm a little worried about.' Rafferty continued. 'There might be something back here that I don't know about, but something somebody else does, although I can't imagine what it might be.'

Baker studied the map carefully, following the canyon bottoms with his fingers, one after another, and noting the places where Rafferty had written in landmark features, like a lightning-struck tree, or an odd-shaped rock, or maybe a slash of colour on a cliff face. It was all there, meticulously rendered.

'Well, boss, let me tell you something,' Baker said. 'It doesn't much matter what they know, or what they want. They were gonna have a fine time separating Hugh Rafferty by himself from something he doesn't care to be separated from. Take an army – and I know an army or two that's tried. Still, you never know. You could trip and hit your head on a stone, and they could sneak by you and grab the place. But this is different. I just don't know how anybody's going to drive off Hugh Rafferty and Quanah Baker *and* Jim Briggs's sharpshooting girl-child. I just don't know how it can be done. And if it *can* be done, I'm glad I'm here to see it, because it'd be a thing to see.'

Rafferty smiled.

'Well, lad, let's tell just a little bit of the truth. We've all lost one or two in our time,' he said.

'Gentlemen,' interrupted Louise. 'Two things: first off, it's dangerous to underestimate an opponent, and in this case, we still don't even know who the opponent is.'

'Granted,' Rafferty said.

'On the other hand, if my daddy told me the truth, you boys might have lost some fights individually or in pairs, but there was never a fight that was lost when Rafferty, Baker and Briggs were all three involved.'

'That might be true, but that was a different Briggs,' Rafferty said. He regretted it the minute the words were out. The girl looked hurt and angry all at once. She walked to the bunk and strapped on her sixgun, and stepped out the door without another word.

CHAPTER ELEVEN

There was silence in the cabin after Louise Briggs had stormed out, and then Baker spoke softly.

'I have a feeling, Hugh Rafferty, that you're in for a surprise. I have a feeling you'll find Louise Briggs has every bit of Jim Briggs in her. And then some.'

'Maybe, Quanah, but she's a woman,' Rafferty said. He was sorry for having said something that had clearly angered her, but he wasn't quite sure why she should have taken it so badly. She was not the crusty old Ranger her dad had been. He looked at the door until Baker spoke up.

'Well, what needs doing, boss?' Baker said. Rafferty pulled his attention from the door and worked a smile onto his face.

'First of all, you old half-breed, you can stop calling me boss. Sounds strange, ain't proper, and I don't like it any more than you like being called "half-breed".'

'I come and help you keep your ranch, you're the boss. You're the man with everything to lose. You come and fight in my fight, and I'll be the boss. As for "half-breed", there's not many men in this country that could call me that without having to pay for their mistake. You, on the other hand, could call me most anything. I've seen you in a fight, and I know that mouth ain't connected to your brain in any normal way, so I wouldn't hold it against you. Besides, while you're keeping people in the dark about whether you're really *the* Rafferty, I might as well not get in the habit of using your real name, right?'

'Enough! Call me anything you want.'

'So what needs doing, boss?'

'We could use some supplies from town, just in case. I didn't get all the things three of us would need when I was in. And it wouldn't hurt to get some information. You might be able to get some that I couldn't.'

'Yeah. The whole town knows I'm in the territory, but they don't know where I stand. Have you got a pack horse without your brand on it? Hard to keep a secret in town if I'm leading RS stock.'

'I traded a fellow for a horse a while back, and I don't believe the town people know about it. You can take that one. I'll round it up and then go after the girl.'

CHAPTER TWELVE

Quanah Baker rode into a hornet's nest.

The ride into town had been uneventful, and he'd had the chance to scout the ways into the RS Connected. Once in Springwater, he went directly to the store and made his purchases with as little discussion as necessary, but keeping his ears open.

He'd finished loading the pack horse with sacks of flour, a good-sized hunk of bacon and assorted supplies when three men came out of the saloon and immediately moved toward him.

There was nothing special about Baker, except he was the only man on the street, and he was dark in colour. For these three, maybe, that was enough. He was tying down the gear when two of them came up, both clearly drunk.

'We saw you in town yesterday,' said one in a red shirt. Baker said nothing and went on checking his lashings. The man spoke again. 'You only had one horse then. How come you got two now?'

Baker ignored the man. The two drunk men wavered a little, and their faces screwed up as they let themselves get offended.

'My friend asked you a question, mister,' said the second. 'Maybe you're just out of Africa. Maybe you don't under-stand English so good, huh? We want you to talk to us, now.

You understand that?'

Baker smiled his most benevolent smile and turned to face the two. He spoke softly enough for them to hear, but so his voice would not carry beyond them.

'You boys think about what you're doing. Think real hard, will you?'

They grinned, pleased to have generated a response. The red-shirted man stood to the left, the other, wearing a dusty leather vest, was just two feet away. A third leaned against the building behind them, appearing too drunk to talk. They looked down on Baker from the boardwalk. It was clear the two speakers were not ready to give up.

'Come on, boy. Where'd you get that horse? You got something to hide, don't you? Tell us about that horse.'

Baker grew very controlled. He watched his position in respect to the two men. He finished tying down the pack horse's gear with his left hand, keeping the right near his pistol and ready for action if it was needed. Quanah Baker was a cautious man. Experience told him that to get into a discussion with these two would be dangerous. He continued trying to ignore them, but they kept at him.

'Answer my friend's question, will ya?' demanded the second man. He raised his voice. 'Where'd a man like you get that horse? I think the whole town might wanna know where that horse came from,' he yelled.

The third man staggered up to the hitching rail, belched and hollered, 'Yeah!'

'I think he's not answering because he don't have an answer. I think he probably stole that horse,' 'Red Shirt' said, in tones equally loud.

Baker turned to face the men.

'If you want to call me a horse thief, you'd best be ready to support your claim.' He spoke quietly, noting that the drunks' loud voices had brought people out onto the street.

'I'm not calling you anything. Just asking a simple

question. Where'd you get that horse? Personally, that horse looks kinda familiar to me. I'd like to know where it came from.'

Baker kicked himself internally. He should have gotten on his horse and led the pack animal away. Now he had spoken and was involved with these men. He had to respond.

'Sir, you're putting me in a very awkward position. If I am a horse thief, then I'd have to fight you to get away from here. If I'm not a horse thief, then I'd have to fight you for calling me one. Do you really want to fight me that badly? You being as drunk as you are?

'Maybe you figured the three of you could just come up and bully a man, have a little fun with a stranger. But the whole town's watching now. You're standing, what, maybe fifteen feet from me there. Your friends are standing right next to you. Maybe you thought I'd try a fist fight, so the three of you could have a nice time with me. Well, I'm going to tell you honestly that I don't like those odds. I prefer three guns to one rather than six fists to two.

'You could hit me with your shot. Hard to miss at this range. And maybe your friend there would help. Your second friend might be able to get his pistol out of his holster in time, and he might not. Now, I believe I can get a shot into each of you before I quit shooting, no matter how much lead I've got in me.

'And I've got these horses I could step behind. Good chance I'd get lead into you, and you'd shoot my horse.

'So what does that get us? It gets us three, maybe four, of us dead or wounded. And all because you came out here and shot your mouth off without thinking.

'Do you want to do some thinking now, mister? How about just walking back into that bar and having another drink. I didn't particularly want to die today, but I suppose it's as good a day for it as any other. How about you? You rather have another whiskey or a piece of lead? I've been talking quietly, so the town doesn't know what I've said to you. You could just nod and walk away, and nobody'd think anything of it. Why don't you do that now? Just walk back to the bar and have one.'

Baker smiled, letting it look like a friendly talk. The town would have heard the drunks' voices, but not his. He turned to the other two.

'What about you other boys? You come out here to die, or just for a breath of air? What do you think?'

Baker stood between his mount and the pack horse. He was in the gunfighter's stance, his hand hanging like a claw over the pistol on his right hip. He let the hand slowly lower toward the grip.

'Myself, I could use a drink,' said the man in the vest, sweating. It broke the tension.

'Yeah, me, too,' said the more drunken one, lurching away from the rail.

The remaining man watched Baker briefly, then joined his friends without a word. Baker waited until they were well inside. He turned from the horses and followed them in. The three stood at the bar, facing the bartender. Baker stepped up beside them.

'I'd like to buy these three men whatever they're drinking, and a whiskey for me,' he said, dropping coins on the bar. The men didn't look his way.

The saloon was still for a good three minutes, waiting for something to happen. When nothing did, the card game in one corner resumed, and conversations picked back up. Baker was about to leave when a hand touched his shoulder.

He turned, and his gun was in his fist.

It was a small man with wiry build and tight curly hair. He wore two pistols, both tied down. The man had been sitting alone at a window table. Baker had checked him out on entering the saloon. The man held his hands away from his sides, indicating he had no intentions of using the guns.

'I don't want you, mister,' he said.

'I hope not. Enough people already have today,' Baker said.

'I saw that. Impressive. Can you shoot as well as you can talk?'

'My pappy always said you shouldn't take a hand at all unless you know how to play the endgame. But you're not here for casual chats about my pappy.'

'Name's Sam Kern. There might be some work. Good money. Fightin' wages.'

'Who do I have to shoot?'

'Don't have to shoot anybody, for sure. Just help a man get some land.'

'That sounds like shooting to me. Whose land is it?'

'Range, and a squatter on part of it. Just one squatter, nothing big. And there are lots of hands on our side, so chances are it wouldn't be you having to shoot anybody.'

'Who would I be working for?'

'Mr Simon. Mr Jack Simon is the man paying the bills. A strong man; the kind of man men follow.'

'I'll tell you the truth. Just now, I'm not looking for work. I'm just doing a little prospecting back there in the hills. Got me a tip,' Baker said.

'You might want to be careful. I hear the squatter is a mite touchy about folks in the area. You'd want to be a part of a big organization if you were gonna go up there. But sure enough, there's word there's gold up there. And that's the good thing. Mr Simon said all he wants is to run some cows on the range. Kind of a retirement deal for him. He's not interested in the gold, and he'd let his men work it on their own.'

'First time I ever heard of somebody not interested in gold. Kinda makes me suspicious.' Quanah picked up the glass the bartender had placed before him on the bar and took a sip of the whiskey.

'A man's gotta do some thinking in the situation like this. Couple of things right off that don't seem to add up. Most folks, when they're ready to retire, they've done their fighting. Never heard of somebody wanted a war over a place to retire. That, and all that gold with only one man in the way. If there's all this gold up there, like you and me heard, how come the squatter hasn't used it to hire his own army?'

'Hard to tell. They say this Rafferty is a recluse. Just digs it himself, doesn't want anybody else around.'

'Just one more question. If this Mr Simon is so good, why doesn't he take Rafferty himself?'

'You want answers to questions like that, Mister, uh. . . .'

'Baker. Call me Baker.'

'Mr Baker, well, you wait until you're on the payroll and you can ask Mr Simon yourself.'

'Right. Well, I'll wait until I see what the country looks like before I take sides, I guess.'

'Suit yourself. Just keep in mind that if it comes to a fight, some of the boys might figure you're agin us, just because you ain't with us.'

'Some of your boys be thinking that way already, seems like. You tell Mr Simon I appreciate his offer, but I'm not in a position to accept just now. And you can tell your boys that if they decide I'm against them, they'd better be in better shape than those boys I talked to outside. They'd better be ready to die,' Baker said, and he pushed past the swinging doors into the street.

He looked around. The people who'd come out to see him deal with the drunks had gone back in. All the folks who'd been on the street when the stage had come in yesterday were back about their business. There was just one man still in sight. A tall man in grey.

That was something to consider. He and Louise Briggs had both noticed the person yesterday who'd spied on them from an upstairs window, and that person had had a grey sleeve. Same shade of grey as this suit. A reasonable assumption was that it was the same person.

Why would the man have been hiding in an upstairs room? Baker considered the possibilities. What was going on just then? Stage coming into town. A stage carried strangers. A stage might also carry an acquaintance; someone who might recognize the man in grey when he didn't want to be recognized. Could be something like that. It suggested that the man had enemies or had something to hide.

But what caught Baker's attention about him today was his guns. They were holstered butt-forward. The man in grey had a cross-draw. Not a common thing. A thing to be remembered.

Baker once more tested his lashings on the pack horse, mounted up and headed out of town, trying to look casual as he peered from side to side under the brim of his hat.

At the edge of Springwater, he turned quickly as if to check the pack horse. He saw that Sam Kern, the man who'd offered him a job in the bar, had crossed the dusty street and was talking to the man in grey. They were looking up the street at Baker as they talked.

Baker nodded, as if satisfied with the pack horse, and headed on out. Kern would have gone to his employer to report the failure to hire a new gunman. Odds, then, were that the man in grey, who might have something to hide, was the mysterious Mr Simon – Jack Simon. It was not a name Baker was familiar with.

All in all, the trip to town had been a success. He'd gotten his supplies and he'd gained a fair amount of information.

The first thing to do now would be to leave no trail. It wouldn't do for Simon and them to know Rafferty had friends. Wouldn't do at all.

CHAPTER THIRTEEN

It was the next morning. Rafferty had reached an uneasy peace with Louise the day before. He rolled out early, quietly fixed the coffee and left the pot on the fire while Louise continued to sleep. Rafferty wasn't used to having people around, and he figured these two could take care of themselves, so he prepared to slip away for the day.

Outside, he threw his saddle on one of the horses and walked it out to where Baker had bedded down by a big tree. The chill of night was still in the air, and the grass was wet with dew or a light night rain. Baker was rolled up in a blanket with a slicker thrown over it, his boots alongside.

Rafferty watched the man, and caught the moment he woke, having heard the rustle of Rafferty and the horse heading through the grass. There was the slightest jerk as he came awake, but then he stayed motionless. Rafferty saw one hand move quickly up under one boot and come up with a pistol. He slipped it back under the blanket and opened an eye.

'Oh, you!' Baker nodded, sliding the pistol back into the holster under his boot.

'There's coffee on. Louise is still asleep – or pretending to be. I've got some thinking to do, and I figure to do some work up at the Stone House. I told you where it was.'

'You did. I'll find a way to stay busy, and Louise said she's got plenty to do around here.'

'See you tonight.'

'Or whenever.'

'Or whenever. See you.'

'Hmm,' Baker said, closing his eyes.

Rafferty swung into the saddle and cut up the valley, pulling on a pair of gloves against the cold. He did his best thinking while he worked, so he headed for the place he called the Stone House. It was a spot he'd selected early on, the place where he wanted to build his permanent house. But it was a big project and would take time. Meanwhile, he'd built and moved into the more convenient cabin down the valley, and worked on the Stone House when he had time.

The morning brightened steadily, but the sun wouldn't break the horizon for someone on the canyon bottom for another three hours. Rafferty rode warily, letting his eyes sweep the spread ahead and pick out potential ambush spots along the sides. He picked out a variety of small wildlife, but no two-legged creatures.

He set the horse loose in a small field off to the left and below the house site. Rafferty shucked his shirt and pulled on a pair of hide gloves to protect his hands from the rough edges and surfaces of the boulders he'd be moving.

Baker had given him the rundown on the events in Springwater. The gunfighters and ruffians were swelling the town's population. All at the behest of this man called Simon. But who was Simon?

CHAPTER FOURTEEN

Big Jim Dunedin worked his way along rocky outcroppings and rested in caves during the worst of the midday heat, protecting himself and his horse. He had travelled hard from before dawn well into the morning, eased off during the midday, and picked up the pace again as the afternoon began to take the sizzle out of the day's heat. Where there was no cover, he would rest a while in the shade of a Joshua tree.

Dunedin's trip through the desert took as direct a course as he could manage, but one drawn off a straight track by the availability of water.

A desert was defined by being arid, but there were places where water could be found. A man with the right information could cross hundreds of miles of desert, while a man without it could easily die in a couple of days.

Dunedin's horse picked its way carefully through the hardy desert shrubbery, avoiding the thorns of the ocotillo, and the cholla and the barrel cacti. He guided the animal where possible along natural trails, keeping away from the shaded areas beneath creosote bushes and other places where rattlers might lie sleeping.

The man's eyes moved constantly, catching the movement of the small desert birds flitting among the vegetation and the shadows of the birds of prey hovering overhead. He spotted the lizards that dashed from his path and pin-pointed the location of fatter chuckwallas, which many a desert dweller had been forced to eat in hard times.

Dunedin watched the tracks. They told him what kinds of animals inhabited an area, but also provided other clues, such as the direction of the nearest waterhole. There were few enough, and often they were days apart. His food stocks were spare, and he could use the addition of some fresh meat.

He found the tracks of desert bighorn sheep near a waterhole. Many desert-dwelling creatures were able to live off the moisture in plants and on the dew, but the sheep needed regular water. A sheep's track was an indication that water was nearby.

This waterhole was in a gully. It was a seep out of the rock at the bottom of the wash. The water pooled on the hard rock, ran downhill a short distance, and then disappeared back into the ground. At morning, the trail of water was some fifteen yards long, but after the desert animals had watered in the pool and the sun had baked the ground, the rivulet dried up just five yards from the seep.

Dunedin watered his horse, then picketed it up the valley and out of sight from the waterhole. He took his rifle and picked a spot well off any game trails. Then he waited. The desert animals knew he was about, and they were wary, but eventually, unable to spot him and doubtless thirsty, they came to the waterhole.

He watched several sheep come to the hole, picked out the one he wanted, and dropped it with a single shot. There was a squawk from the desert birds, and then silence. He waited to see if there was any other reaction to the shooting. He heard and saw nothing amiss. Dunedin got up and walked quickly to the carcass, cutting away the pieces he wanted.

His canteens were full, and he walked with his supply of

meat to the horse, which had been grazing on a sparse patch of sub-irrigated grass. They covered several miles before he stopped to fry up some of the meat. He watered his horse from his canteens by pouring water into his hat, and letting the animal drink from it. After cooking and eating, he was up and riding once more.

The mountain man rode as long into the twilight as he could see a safe track. The country was open, and he gained a few additional miles by starlight before settling in for the night.

He was up and moving again before dawn.

CHAPTER FIFTEEN

On his last trip to the Stone House, Rafferty had hauled a load of rock from a slide a hundred yards up the valley. He'd built a sled of heavy, smooth runners and cross braces. His horse would pull it to the work site. He'd unloaded the rocks and laid the sled up on its side, so its beams wouldn't rot from the moisture of the soil. Now he got to work setting the individual stones.

Simon. John Simon. The name didn't ring a bell, but that wasn't so unusual. Men used a variety of names in the West, and for a variety of reasons. They sought anonymity to escape past embarrassments, to escape criminal punishments, or even to escape glory. A famous man, whether he gained his fame through good deeds or bad, often had reason to wish for peace and quiet. But people sought out the famous. A name change was the easiest way to foil those people. A change of location helped. A change of appearance did more. And a change in the way a man behaved could be the ultimate hiding place. Unfortunately, people had difficulty changing the way they acted. A bad man under one name was generally just as bad under another.

Rafferty had staked out the corners of the house and had done some preliminary work there, but mainly now he was building the approaches to the house. The place was set on a hill, and had a commanding view of much of the valley below. Rafferty now was building retaining walls on the slope leading up to the homesite.

John Simon was sure not to be the man's real name. There were few enough men in this part of the country, and not all that many in the entire West. The men with drive, the ones who led others, whether they stole or they built, were known. For a country so spread out, it was remarkable how quickly word got around. The spoken word was just about the only form of communication, and people were good at it. Stories were told in every meeting place. Strangers were sought out for their information. An out-of-work cowboy in a bar would drop a story about a gunfight, or a gold find, and four people would hear it. Two might move on to another town, repeating the story. A few more would take it further. Men passing on the trail could give it another push, and the story might get to the most distant part of the country nearly as quickly as a man might have carried it there directly. So if neither Rafferty nor Baker had heard of a gunfighter or ringleader named John Simon, it just stood to reason that John Simon wasn't the man's name. Rafferty and Baker had been around.

There were things to be considered in building the stone retaining walls. If they were vertical, then they could provide shelter to a man attacking the main house. A man lying at the base of such a wall would be invisible from the house on the hill. So most of the walls sloped upward. Rafferty took a pick and a shovel he kept at the Stone House. The first job was to dig a shallow trench to hold the base course of stones, which would support all the others. He set to work digging. He enjoyed the feeling that hard work brought to his back and muscles. He warmed up with the earth moving and got into a rhythm. Select the spot. Poke the shovel. Push it down. Lift up. Toss the dirt. Swing back. Select a spot. Over and over. It was steady work that let him think. And right now, he needed to think.

84

If he worked on the assumption that John Simon was an alias, as he was sure it was, then what was the man's real name? He knew little enough about the man. Baker had said Kern had gone across the street to confer with a man in grey. That man almost certainly would have been Simon. A man could change clothes, and if he were trying to hide his identity, he surely would. So the grey clothing meant nothing. But Baker had said he looked somewhat the dandy. His clothes were well cared for, the shirt properly tucked in. Sure enough, a man changed his clothes, but not his habits. A slovenly man would not suddenly begin changing the customs of a lifetime. If he was natty now, he would have been before.

And the guns? The cross-draw? There was something a man surely wouldn't change. When you learned to use a gun, finally, you used it without thinking. The hand was trained to grab it, lift and shoot. You didn't dare move a low-slung gun higher on the hip, for fear the hand would get a bad grip on the draw. It could cost a gunman his life. And you wouldn't switch a conventional draw for a cross-draw. So he knew that much about the man who called himself Simon. A fancy dresser and a cross-draw. It narrowed the prospects. For some reason, Rafferty's thoughts went to riverboats and gamblers.

Rafferty had placed poles upright in the ground where the windows of the Stone House would be. Cross pieces were tied to the poles at window height. Then he went to the site of a retaining wall and put a long, straight stick to the ground at the base of the proposed wall. He aimed the stick like a rifle at the cross pieces, and stuck it firmly into the ground. Another stick at the other end of the wall was placed in the same way. The plane formed by the sticks was the slope of the stone wall. A man lying at the base of the wall thus would be fully visible from the Stone House, preventing sneak attacks. Rafferty had his sticks in the ground.

Now he sighted along each of them to make sure the angle was right. He braced them, and was ready to begin hauling rocks.

Gold. That could be it. The gunmen wanted gold and Simon wanted a place to retire. Well, there wasn't much gold to be had on this spread. Not unless a man wanted to do a lot of work, and even then nothing was for sure. Rafferty had been in the country enough times to know. A little pocket here, a bit of colour there, but nothing to suggest a large find. Most of the gold the town of Springwater had seen come from Rafferty had been gold he'd brought to support the ranch until it could make some money of its own. He hadn't spent much, and there was precious little left. If there had been plenty of gold, he'd certainly not have been working this hard. In fact, it was precisely because of the lack of gold, the broken cattle country and the isolation of this place that Rafferty wanted it. He wanted a quiet place to work and be left alone. In his own way, he was escaping a reputation just as John Simon must be.

In the proper design of a house or a castle, you looked at all the eventualities you could think of. There might come a time when the Stone House was taken, whether because its occupants were away or because they had finally been driven out, and Rafferty would then want to change roles and be the attacker. He had thought about that, and had developed designs for that, too. There were isolated routes up the slope through which an approach might be made out of sight of the house. A slight bulge in a wall here, a short jog there, provided cover. But the spots were selected and built so they didn't look like cover. It would take a man quite a time to locate them if he didn't know they were there. You never knew when you might need an edge, and Rafferty gave himself the edge when he could. That was how you lived to be an old gunfighter. There weren't many around. Rafferty intended to be one. He hoisted a boulder into the trench, dropping it into place so its weight would leave a depression in the earth. He took note of the angle of its upper surface. Now he rolled it out of the way, glancing at the bottom of the rock and then at the compacted area its bottom had made in the trench. He dug a depression in the trench to match its bottom, and one that would leave its upper surface fairly flat, a secure base for the next course of stones. He rolled the boulder back, and it settled down with a satisfying thump. Rafferty put his arms around it and twisted until it was seated firmly. Pebbles and earth were jammed around it in places where his hole hadn't fit perfectly. Now he stood on it and stepped around the edges to be sure it held firm. It did. He went to his rock pile to select the next one.

What did John Simon really want with this country? It just didn't make sense. You couldn't run enough cattle up here to have any kind of a fancy ranch. You couldn't justify more than one or two hands most of the time. And it was a place that required work. Any fool could see it wasn't the kind of a place you'd pick to retire. Any fool, Rafferty thought, but me. That's what I'm doing here, retiring, in a sense. Fine, but Baker's description of John Simon didn't match the picture you might draw of the kind of man for this range. There had to be something else, some other reason for his wanting the RS Connected. It wasn't gold, and it probably wasn't retirement. What was it?

Rafferty was moving his fourth big boulder into position when he heard his horse nicker. He looked up and saw the animal facing down the slope. Rafferty was wearing his gunbelt. Whatever it was, he was ready. He had time, and finished setting the fourth rock. He rolled two more likely candidates up alongside the trench, and then got down behind his pile of rocks, in a comfortable sitting position, his rifle supported on a granite block. He checked his horse again to see if it had detected anything else. He slowly scanned the terrain in a full circle, and returned his attention to the valley floor.

A rider appeared far below. The first thing Rafferty recognized was one of his own horses. That horse had been in the paddock by the cabin. Was something amiss? He studied the scene. A small rider. As they worked their way up toward the house site, the details grew clearer. Finally Rafferty recognized Louise. She was dressed like a man, with Colt on her hip and her hair caught up under her hat. Rafferty took another scan of the surroundings, detecting nothing amiss. He came up from behind the rock pile. In the time it would take her to arrive, he could get another foundation stone settled. He lifted it, his back straight and hauling it up with the strength of his legs. He could feel a light breeze on his bare back, blowing up the slope, and he imagined he could smell something of Louise in that wind. The woman smell she had brought into the cabin. She was the first woman who'd ever been there. As far as he knew, she was the first white woman ever to set foot on this country.

The stone set, he turned to find her just twenty yards away. Her horse's head bobbed as it stepped among the stones approaching Rafferty. He noted a lather, and knew it wasn't all from the difficulty of the climb up to the site. Louise had been running this horse, and even though the day wasn't warm, the horse was hot and tired.

She climbed down and began to speak, but he stopped her.

'Hold on a minute,' he said.

He pulled the saddle off her horse and efficiently wiped it down with the blanket. Done, he turned the horse loose, and it trotted over to the pasture to join his own mount. These horses had been raised together. They nuzzled each other, and both went to cropping the grass.

CHAPTER SIXTEEN

'Rafferty, there's been killing,' Louise said.

'I expected it would start soon enough. Who caught it?'

'I was out riding, getting the lay of the land down at the entry to your valley. I was down near the place where the stream takes a pair of switchbacks, and I thought I saw smoke up against a bluff a couple of miles off to the right.'

'That'd be the Blake place. Young couple, out of Pennsylvania. They had a few cows, but he hoped to do some farming, sell grain and vegetables to the ranchers. Can't hardly get good fresh supplies at any reasonable price, unless you grow them yourself. He's had some trouble, what with a drought and some varmints, but I think it's a good scheme and it could work for him.'

'Not any more, Hugh. He's dead. They're both dead.'

'What?'

'Killed. Like I said, I saw the smoke. I followed it up, figuring it might be somebody's fire. I figured to nosey up and see what they were about, in case it was rustlers. . . .'

'That's awful dangerous for a woman, Louise. You oughtn't to be wandering around the country alone in any case, and you sure shouldn't be going into places where it could be dangerous.'

'I can take care of myself just fine, Hugh Rafferty! Anyway, I came up and realized it was more than a campfire.

It was a cabin gone.'

'What? The Blake place?'

'If that's their names, I guess so. There was a fenced field, where the ground was tilled. I found a man there. He was dead. Shot through the chest next to his plough. And Hugh, he wasn't armed! Shot in cold blood. There didn't seem to be anyone around, so I went up to the house. There wasn't much left, just the smoking ruins and the chimney still standing.

'I found what was left of the woman where the porch must have been. I guess she'd faced them and they shot her down. She had a shotgun still gripped in her hands. She'd taken three rounds, one in the belly and one in the neck, and then another one into the back after she was down!'

'I talked to those folks only last week,' Rafferty said. 'Mel Blake was real excited. His crops were doing okay and he was getting set for the winter. Said his wife figured she was pregnant. It was all going right for them, after a tough start. They were just real nice folks, hoping to raise a family in this country.'

'I did some detective work, Hugh. Figured to get a hint of who did it. One thing, she got two shots off. I found the shells, one on the ground next to her and one still in the shotgun. She had an apron on, with a handful of shells in it, too. She was ready for bear.

'Well, one of those shots, the last one, she must have fired while she was falling. You could see the impression of the shot in the dirt about six feet in front of her. She got the other one off, got some buckshot into somebody. I found a few drops of blood on the ground.'

'Probably the one she shot was so mad, he was the one that fired into her body after she fell. Did you track the attackers by the hoofprints?'

'I did. They came on the man first, shot him without even dismounting. She must have heard the shots and gotten the shotgun before coming out of the house. The tracks show three horses were walked up to the house. My guess is they had words and she lifted the shotgun and fired, then they pulled on her, or one did. I don't know too many men who would pull a gun on a woman and shoot her, and then keep shooting after she'd fallen. That takes a special kind of man, Hugh.'

'A dangerous man, an unstable one. What happened then? Did the tracks lead into the house, as if they were looking for something?'

'Nope, they weren't looking for anything. The injured man stayed on his horse. The other two got down and lit fires in two places around the cabin. They never went inside or walked near her body. Then they mounted up and left. I got there, must have been, a couple of hours later. There wasn't anything to do, so I figured to come and tell you about it.'

'Anything special about the sign these men left? The hoofprints?'

'No, I didn't see anything to make a note of, but there was one thing. One of the men who got down and burned the house had a deep cut in the right heel of his boot. I'd recognize it again, a diagonal cut right through the first layer of leather on the heel.'

'That's good to know. Gives us something we can identify them by. One man took some lead, and another with the cut boot.'

'There was something else, Hugh. A fourth man. Four riders came up to the place, but one stopped down near the lowest fence line. He waited there while the shooting and firing got done, and then the three killers joined him as they left.'

'Likely the man that sent them. Didn't want to do the dirty work himself. Makes him a coward, or a very careful man. There's not much risk in killing innocent folks most times, but there's always some. A woman can up with a shotgun and surprise you.'

Rafferty had Louise Briggs help him do the sighting for the framework of another stone wall while her horse rested. The sun was falling below the peaks overhead when they headed back for the cabin.

'Quanah and I will go bury the Blakes in the morning. Their range wasn't much, but it covered the main approach to the RS Connected. You could keep track of most of the entrances to my range from parts of theirs. If someone wanted that kind of control, it might make sense to get the Blakes out of the way,' Rafferty said, thinking aloud.

'This is more than just someone wanting pasture. This is someone wanting absolute control over a big part of this part of the country. Someone wants to be sure they can operate in private, without any curious onlookers. Puts a little different light on Simon, Kern and their boys, I'd guess.

'I'd guess, too, that this means they're taking the fight into the open. Up to now, they've been happy with drygulching work, but they must have their army ready to go. Could be the next battle won't be one or two guns. It could be open warfare,' he said.

They were silent for more than a mile of riding in the gathering darkness. He picked a trail up along the edge of the cliffs so he'd have a view by moonlight of the valley below, where attackers might expect him to go. That was where the main trail was, the one cattle tended to take when they were moving, and one he had often used when riding his range.

'What happens now, Hugh?' Louise said.

'We won't have to wait long to find out, I'd wager. These boys, whatever their motivation is, will be bringing it to us. They want my range, and they want it bad. I suspect they'd like to be in control before the snow falls, because it's no kind of country to be fighting in during winter. Snow piles up yards high back here and it gets colder than any creature would deal with of his own choice.'

'What'll you do?'

He rode a while, thinking about that before responding.

'I'll stay, and I'll fight.' Rafferty was comfortable with Louise riding nearby. He felt talkative, and since she was a friend of long standing, someone who'd known him most of his adult life, he went on.

'In my time, I've fought for most everybody else. For Texas, for individual settlers, for the railroads. I've fought Injuns and outlaws and Mexicans, and killed a few, all for other folks.

'Now I've come here to build my own place. All that fighting before, that helped other people build their futures. I finally got tired of that, tired of being a hired gun, which is what it is when you fight on the side of the law just the same as if you work for an outlaw. You just feel better about it if the community supports you. I had enough of it, though, and I came here to stop fighting and to start building something of my own. Any kind of place you build, if you produce something folks need, whatever it might be, you're helping to build the whole area, the territory and in the long run, the nation. I just got tired of fighting and not building. I wanted something to keep me when I got older, and I wanted the feeling that I was adding something to this country, instead of just keeping other folks from tearing it down. There's a place for a lawman, no question, but I had enough of that.

'Now come Simon and his bunch, and they figure they can make better use of this country than I can. Well, if they'd come up and made me a good offer, and convinced me the country would be better off with them in charge than me, at least I'd have thought about it. But they didn't. They tried to take it. That's something else, and I don't know if they realize it or not, but it's something I know how to handle.

'There's more to running a ranch than knowing how a cow works. There might be lots of folks know more about cows than me, when it comes to keeping the land those cows walk on, when it comes to protecting it, well, I know something about that. I've spent my life fighting to protect land, in one way or another. Now it's my own land I'm protecting, and that makes me more determined. Simon and them, they just don't know what it is they've tied into. But if they keep coming, they'll sure as shooting find out,' he said.

Rafferty stopped talking, suddenly aware of how much he'd said, and embarrassed by it. Louise stole a glance at the man, riding straight in the saddle as he did, his eyes ever moving in the moonlight, alert as any wild animal; not fearful but strong, assured. He'd worked hard on the rocks at the Stone House, and should have been exhausted. If he was, he didn't show it. There was a deep strength in the man, a fortitude. He was everything she'd remembered about him, and more. As attractive a man as she could remember ever knowing. They arrived at the cabin to find food ready. Quanah had prepared biscuits and stew. Wolf loped out to greet them, leaving the bones Quanah had given him. The big dog had already cracked several to get at the marrow. Once the horses were cared for and the three were inside, he returned to them. Louise, Rafferty and Quanah Baker could hear the cracking of the bones outside as they ate.

In the morning Baker and Rafferty found the situation at the Blakes' place as Louise Briggs had described it. They dug a wide grave on a hill off to the side, overlooking Mel Blake's beloved fields. They'd found a blanket for his wife's body. It was partly burned in the cabin fire. They wrapped her up in it and lowered her into the hole next to her husband. Rafferty filled the grave while Quanah Baker carved the cross for the head of the mound. Before they left, Baker scratched a few words into another cross he placed at the foot. The words read:

3 AGINST ONE,
AND HE HAD NO GUN.
KILT HER TOO.

'That gets around, it should fire a few people up,' Baker said as they rode away. A mile along the trail, Rafferty pulled up at the sight of a pair of cows.

'Wait a minute, Quanah. This looks strange. I'd swear those are my cows, but look at this brand.'

Rafferty got his rope out and put a loop over one of them, tying it off to a tree. He inspected the brand.

'This is a new brand, Quanah, but it's not the first one this cow's had. What do you think of it?'

'Cloverleaf. I've seen it used as a rustler's brand. It covers your RS Connected almost perfectly. You sure you know this cow?'

'I am now. A wolf got its mother, and I had to lead it around until I could find another cow to take over until it went from milk to grass. This one's mine all right. Let's take a look around. Blake had a few cows that wandered around this area, too.'

'What's his brand?'

'Just the letter B, for Blake. Nothing fancy.'

'Cloverleaf would cover that, too.'

They rode for three hours, crisscrossing the country. There were still a few RS Connected, but they found no cattle with the Blake brand. Many of the brands were new ones, just a day or two old.

'I'll tell you something, Rafferty. Not a single cow we've seen shows evidence of a long trail ride. You know what that means?'

'Sure. No new cattle here. Somebody just waltzed in and began branding everything in sight.'

'And they've already gotten all the Blake cattle. Means they started on his before they killed him. Now they've started on yours.'

'So somebody's out to kill me. Tell me something I didn't know, Quanah. Could begin to get a little warm hereabouts. This is my fight, and you don't have to take a hand in it. You could take Louise and head out of here.'

'Two things wrong with that kind of thinking. I'd like to see the man that could take Louise any place she doesn't want to go, and I can assure you she won't be interested in leaving. The other thing is that I think you may need a hand around here when it comes to rebranding your cows, so maybe I'll just hang around.'

CHAPTER SEVENTEEN

Rafferty saddled his favourite old bay mare, a feisty horse, but a smart one. She'd expand her belly when he tightened the cinch, so it would be more comfortable later. It also meant the saddle tended to slip. Rafferty waited until she exhaled to pull it tight. The horse had a dainty step, but a sure one that moved quickly over the roughest terrain.

He had about fifteen cows with his best bull up a small canyon two hours' ride from the cabin. It was the core of his breeding herd, and several of the cows should be ready to drop their young. He headed that way to check on them.

The problems with the outsiders might occupy much of his time, but he still had a ranch to run. The events of the last few days ran through his mind as he rode.

There were tracks in the valley. Fresh tracks. They seemed to lead into the canyon that was his destination. He stopped as he turned up the canyon. There was dust in the air. Something more than the normal stuff raised by the movement of the cows.

There was little cover for a mounted man for 200 yards. Rafferty dropped to the ground and led his horse. The horse's movement wouldn't be out of place if spotted, and Rafferty himself was well protected by the brush he walked through. He stopped. The sound of men working was up ahead. He caught voices in the stillness of the day. Was there a lookout?

He climbed back into the saddle, noted it was a little loose, and dropped off to tighten the cinch. Back up, he moved forward, keeping to a line that maintained several trees between him and the spot from which the sound came. He pulled up behind a clutch of low pines and dropped from the horse again. He stroked its face and whispered, dropping the reins around a bough.

Rafferty moved forward in spurts, staying low in the humus of rotted branches and needles. If there was a lookout, he couldn't spot it, and the men were incautious. They didn't stop to listen, and were so full of their own sounds that they missed a loud crack of a branch under Rafferty's knee.

He'd seen what he needed. Rafferty backed up along the crawl route he'd used coming in, turning and standing at the trees' dripline. He mounted, checked his guns, and rode around the copse to face them.

There were six men working his cows. They had a couple of calves down, and a herd of thirty or so cattle backed up a small draw. They'd apparently driven some of his common stock out of the main valley and up his breeding canyon.

The six were hard at work when Rafferty rode up.

'You boys played hell,' he said. 'Rustling's a shooting crime in these parts.'

The men jerked around as one. They hadn't seen him ride up. One of them, likely the leader, hitched up his pants and took a step forward.

'Don't know what you're talking about, mister. Simon's got title to this ranch, and these cows are his. We're just putting his brand on the young stock and cleaning up any old brands on the other cows.'

The other men walked up around their leader, advancing

on Rafferty, who sat still on the mare. He had a hand on his gun butt, and none of them was going to beat him to a draw, if it came to that.

'Seems to me, boys, that you've been doing more wandering around than branding. By the look of your tracks, you've been searching the territory like a bunch of newcomers. Not the kind of behaviour a man would expect from riders who worked for the man that owned the land.'

'It's not your business to tell us how to do ours, mister,' the leader said.

'Well, we have a little difference of opinion there, gentlemen. I'm the man with title to this land, and if this Simon says he has title, he's lying or somebody's taken him. Now, I'm not a spiteful man. You've had your chance to see some of the country hereabouts. I'll let you mosey back the way you came.'

One of the riders shrugged and moved toward their horses.

'Shucks,' he said. 'No sign of gold around here anyhow.'

'Simon and Kern guaranteed it. It's got to be right around here someplace. This guy's just got it hidden,' said a second. He stayed facing Rafferty, but took a step to the side, separating him from his leader by four feet.

Rafferty kept his attention on the leader. If anything started, he was likely to be the one to start it. And he did. The man grabbed for his gun with the words, 'We're wasting time.'

Rafferty was quicker. His pistol bucked and the man fell back, his own shot kicking up dust at his feet. The others were taken by surprise, their pistols still in their holsters. Rafferty now eased his rifle out of its scabbard and covered the remaining five with both weapons.

'I'm leaving,' said the man who'd first gone for his horse. He kept his hands half raised so there was no chance Rafferty would think he was going for a gun.

'C'mon, boys. There's no gold here, and that Simon says he wants to be a rancher, but he's no cattleman, that's for sure,' he said. A couple of the others eyed Rafferty as if they were willing to give him a try, but finally all turned toward the horses, which were tied in the shade under a pair of trees. 'You boys bring your boss's horse and toss him over it. I don't want his carcass on my ranch,' Rafferty said.

He kept his guns out as they mounted, and followed them with the barrels as they passed close to him, heading down the canyon. The cowboy who'd first walked away from the crowd dallied, and was the last one. He stopped in front of Rafferty.

'I'm done with Simon and Kern, Rafferty. Ya won't see me again. I don't know what they want with this place, anyhow. Ya couldn't never build a good-sized herd up here. Country's too rough and there ain't enough of it that ain't lying on edge. But I heard them talking about some trails they heard about. Trails out of some of these gullies back here. I give you that, for what it's worth. I figure you had us cold, and you could have picked us off. I owed it to you.'

'Thanks,' Rafferty said. 'But if there were any trails out of here, I'd know about it. Those fellows are wrong. There aren't.'

But were there? There were all those light lines on his map, places he hadn't yet explored.

CHAPTER EIGHTEEN

A high mist, just at the treetops, made the world seem to close in. The morning air was chill and dead. The only sounds Rafferty heard were the exaggerated creaks and groans of the saddle, and the clicks of the horse's hoofs.

It was a long, lonesome ride to the RS Connected.

Rafferty pondered his situation. The ranch was naturally fenced. The entrances were formed by two narrow passes bounded by cliffs on both sides. Cattle didn't much wander in and out, and the openings were easily defended. The trouble, Rafferty knew, was that without a back way out, the ranch was a fine fort, but also a trap. Under attack, it could lock its occupants in.

It was good and clear that if there was another way out of this country, he'd better find out about it.

He found Quanah Baker working some pine poles for an extra corral. Three people living and working out of the cabin put a demand on the place for more horses that could be kept near at hand and fed properly. Rafferty's one-man operation wasn't big enough, and Baker, a craftsman, had taken it upon himself to do the expansion. It was a case of a man doing what he, among those available, did best. Baker worked the axe with grace, swinging easy strokes that cut the poles so the tenon ends would fit the mortises he'd chiselled into the posts with Rafferty's two-inch chisel and mallet. The careful work was for the beams on both sides of the gate, where the simpler joinery of the running pole corral sides wouldn't do.

Rafferty filled him in on the morning's activities and hunched with him over the map of the ranch.

'These are the places I haven't explored. I've been in some of them, chasing cattle, or hunting, but the ones I've noted I haven't really studied. What I'm looking for is a way up out of the valley. There are several places where a man could make it on foot, climbing, but I'm thinking of a place where you could take a horse. Maybe an old Injun trail. If Simon is interested in the place and knows about trails out, then he's interested in more than cattle.

'I'd like you to spend some time wandering back there. Look into the back canyons. You could track a ghost over a lava field. Look for any old horse tracks or antelope trails that might lead up the cliffs,' Rafferty said.

Baker nodded.

'And what'll you be doing?'

'I've got some business in town,' Rafferty said.

Once they'd eaten and Baker had begun his ride, Rafferty was ready. It was time to take it to them. He sat on a bench in front of his cabin. The big dog lay at his feet. With a rag he carefully cleaned his pistols, and then went over the workings of the rifle he would take along. He pulled each shell from his gunbelt, inspected it and slipped it back into its loop.

There was no law in Springwater. It was too small a town to afford to hire a sheriff. And it still lacked enough of the kind of sturdy folk that made a town last and that demanded it lose its wilder ways. Marshals came in from neighbouring areas, generally when they were chasing law-breakers on the run. That might have been one of the reasons Simon had selected the area. It was a place where raw power still worked, where the strong survived because

the weaker or more civilized folk hadn't yet grown to suffi-
cient numbers and hadn't joined forces to establish the
rules of the society.

That wasn't to say a tough man could ride roughshod
over the folks in a town like Springwater. Too many of the
residents, the vast majority of whom were men, were hard-
bitten veterans. They'd left the East and been taught tough
lessons on how to survive. The West, too, taught those
lessons. Many had fought in the war between the states or in
wars with the Indians. They knew how to use their guns and
they used them well. They also kept them close at hand.

But the townsfolk weren't being directly threatened by
Simon and his gang. If he made the mistake of trying something in town, he'd have a problem. But he was working
here in a place the town residents hardly considered civilized. They wouldn't likely come to the defence of small
ranchers who were being pushed by a tough bunch. They
had their own problems. If Hugh Rafferty were to beat this
thing, he'd have to do it on his own. It was his ranch, the RS
Connected, and it was arguable that if he couldn't keep it,
he didn't deserve to have it. The strong survived. That was
the way of the West.

The scrape of the cabin door announced Louise stepping outside. Quanah Baker was off studying the gullies and
canyons of the RS Connected, and looking for signs of
rustled cattle. Rafferty and Louise Briggs were the only ones
in the area. He didn't turn as she pushed the door back in
place. The rude panel hung on leather straps for hinges,
but it fit the doorway snugly so the winter blizzards didn't
blow in. Pulled tight, it let no daylight in, but during the
warmer months, it was just wedged enough that light winds
didn't send it swinging. Wolf looked up, exhaled and
dropped his snout to his paws.

'What have you been working on, Louise? You've been
hunched over those leather scraps for the past two days,'

Rafferty said, finishing the work on the rifle with an oiled rag that left a light coat sheen on the barrel.

'I don't want you to get mad, Rafferty. I made something for you. Call it a birthday present if you like.'

'Well, shucks, you didn't have to do that. Nothing I need, anyway,' he said.

'There's more than one thing you need, Hugh Rafferty, but one thing at a time. I made you these,' she said, handing him a pair of moccasins. The leather was soft and supple, as it should have been. The thongs that held it together were sewn tightly and evenly. He turned them over in his hands. Any Western man worth his salt made himself moccasins now and then. Rawhide worked, but was difficult to work with and made uncomfortable footwear. Nicely tanned hide was best, and fresh hides, while soft and comfortable, didn't last long. These were made of properly tanned leather.

'These are fine looking. As good as any squaw-made I've seen,' he said. 'You didn't need to.'

'No, I know that. I wanted to. Try them on.'

Rafferty pulled off his boots and slipped on the mocs, first the left, then the right.

'What's this lump in the heel of the right one?' he said.

'Don't ask. Just stand up and walk around in it, see how it feels.'

He got up, and recognized at once what she'd done. The pad in the heel matched the indentation of the bullet that had crippled him. It fit, and instead of the leg acting like it was shorter than the other, it worked properly.

He walked around and around, trying leaning back, trying walking with a crouch.

'What do you think? Is it comfortable enough?' She looked worried.

'It's just fine. I don't know what to say. It feels perfect. How in blazes did you do it?'

'Well, I saw you limping, and I could tell you weren't comfortable. I know you used to like to walk and run a lot, too. Daddy told me once about a time you literally ran a bank robber down when you were Rangers.'

'Well, me and my horse. A couple of times I got off and ran alongside the horse to give him a break. It gave me the edge on the man running his horse into the ground,' Rafferty said.

'Well, it pained me to see you not being able to, so I tried to figure out something. You didn't look like you were hurting, just that the heel came down wrong, so I figured if I could build up the heel of a moccasin, and use the softest leather to make it fit the hole in your heel, you might be able to move normally.'

Rafferty didn't have anything to say. He pulled the ties tight on the mocs and lit off at an easy jog. Wolf was up in a second, romping alongside. They cut down a path and to the left, dropped across a grassy hillside, then turned and sprinted to the top. Winded, Rafferty walked back to the cabin, rocking back and forth, testing the pad in the shoe.

'It's just great! Going uphill I'm on my toes anyway, so it doesn't make much difference, but on the flats and down-hill, the pad just brings the ground right up to the heel, rather than that heel having to drop an extra inch or two to reach the ground and throwing my stride off.

'I don't know how to thank you for this. An old sock never did much but fill up the space, and it just col-lapsed under pressure. This actually seems to replace the missing part. How did you get the impression of my heel?'

'I didn't know if I could do it, and I knew you wouldn't let me study your foot. The other day you had to clean out the waterhole, and you took off your boots to stand in the mud and work. I found several good impressions in the clay at the edge of the hole. I cut two of them out with a knife. One, I let dry. The other one, I was real careful and carved away the outside, leaving the part that represented the missing part of your heel. I compared it with the other one to make sure I hadn't altered it while working on it. Finally, I made a plug of leather a little smaller than that, and covered it with a piece of thin, soft leather. Then I sewed it into the moccasins.

'If it works with the moccasins, it should work with the boots. I made a little pad to try in your boots. But you should wear this for a while and see if it has any bumps or edges in the wrong places,' she said.

'Louise, this feels just fine. I figure I'm going to have to be careful to let the callouses build up gradually. The heel feels a little tender now, but it should be fine after a couple of weeks. You'll have to show me how you did it, so I can make my own when these wear out,' he said.

'I can always make more for you, Hugh.' She looked at him strangely.

'I mean after you've gone,' he said, not noticing her look.

'That might be quite a while, Hugh Rafferty.'

He heard her and looked up. She was just a girl, after all, the daughter of an old friend. But what he saw when he looked wasn't a girl, but a woman. A woman old enough to be a man's wife. Old enough to bear his children. But that man should be a young man, Rafferty told himself. A vibrant young woman like Louise deserved a young man. She didn't need to be hanging around with old timers like him and Baker. Shouldn't have to. She was a fine looking woman. Fine looking, he thought, and looked away.

It was time to mount up. He got up and caught a big black out of the corral. Still thinking of the girl, he rubbed the horse down and threw up the blanket and saddle. In a minute, he was riding out.

He'd have to talk to her. It was mighty comfortable having her around. A man could get soft having a woman around, but he had a responsibility for her, due to his friendship with her father. She needed to get on with her life, and doing chores around Rafferty's place wasn't going to help much.

He told himself over and over that he should get rid of her, and weighed it against the equally strong argument that she needed a home base, and that the RS Connected was about the only home the girl had, now that her folks were gone.

He was still working it out when the blow knocked him from the saddle. It felt like his head had been knocked off. A single rifle shot, from a distance. He heard the shot just before he hit the ground. He landed like a rag doll, crumpled up, face in the dirt, caught on one shoulder and on his knees, his hips in the air. And then the paralysis and gravity joined up to drop him flat to the ground, semi-conscious, feeling like syrup just spreading out, as low as possible.

He heard the hoofs coming up as if in a dream, and the voices, just two of them.

'Fine shot, Mister Kern. One shot and you caught him right in the head. Couldn't ask for finer shooting.'

'The man has a better reputation than that. He should have been alert, should have known we were there.'

'Don't matter, Mister Kern. It just don't matter what his reasons were, or why he wasn't paying attention. Just shows that you got to send the best against the best. Mister Simon is just going to be right pleased. Do you think we should put a couple more shots into him, just to be safe?'

'There's no pride in desecrating a corpse, John. Leave him be, and people will find him. The evidence of a single, well-placed shot will be considerably more telling than a body shot to ribbons.'

CHAPTER NINETEEN

They rode away. Rafferty lay there a long time, moving nothing, and finally it was dark. He knew hours had passed, and that his mind still worked. But his body remained weak. He tried to open an eye, but it stuck closed. He pushed his hands up under him and tried to rise. The arms lacked the strength.

'Little by little, Rafferty,' he told himself. He pulled a finger up to his face and broke the layer of caked blood. The eye opened. Now the other. He was lying on his face in the dust. He rolled to his back, and putting his hands under himself, pushed to a sitting position. It made him dizzy. He closed his eyes again.

Damn! Shot in the head for the second time. One of these days those people would realize what a hard head he had. Right now, though, it was a sore head, a mighty sore head. The first shot had scabbed over and was well on its way to healing, and now this.

The black was standing fifty yards away, watching him, wary of the smell of blood.

'Come on, boy. Come on over, fella,' he said. The horse seemed interested, but still wary. He called again, and it took a few steps. Finally, the animal came to within a few feet. Rafferty crawled over, grabbed a stirrup and pulled himself to his feet. He could feel a lot of blood caked on his

108

face, but there wasn't much on the ground. The slug had gone in along his right temple. He felt the side of his head, and found a second wound four inches back. That was it, then. It had entered, but had not penetrated the skull. The bullet had ridden under the skin a few inches and exited at the back of his head. He'd lost little blood, and the weakness was the result mainly of a concussion. That would pass.

Rafferty sagged against the side of the horse. He was weak as a kitten, but there was steel down deep. There were times when you just didn't worry about whether you were near the limits of your abilities. You just ignored that and did what needed to be done. Knowing the condition of his wound made Rafferty feel better. It hadn't killed him, and it most likely wouldn't kill him. That being the case, he had to go on. He steadied himself against the mare and carefully slipped his foot into the stirrup. He took a breath, pulled himself into the saddle, overcame a bout of nausea and headed back toward the cabin.

The bay, feisty as she could be, knew there was something wrong, and didn't try any tricky stuff. She treated him like a precious cargo, stepping easily along. Rafferty swayed weakly in the saddle, but he remained alert. As he came up on the cabin, he sensed something was wrong. When he arrived, he knew.

The door was open as he rode up.

A chair was overturned.

A table had been moved, and there were drops of blood on the floor.

Louise was gone.

They'd taken her!

109

CHAPTER TWENTY

This was it then. There was no longer just a question of facing them and convincing them to leave, although that almost certainly would have ended in a shooting battle anyway. He'd track them down, the men who'd taken Louise, and he'd kill them.

Where was Baker? He'd sent the man to look for trails out of the canyons, and as much as Quanah liked sleeping out in the country, he'd probably be a day or two out there. There was no reason he'd need to check back on the cabin, knowing Louise could take care of herself pretty well and that Rafferty was expected back soon enough to be with her.

Rafferty leaned up against the cabin door, his head pounding where the bullet had hit him. He tried to make out the sign the kidnappers left in the dust before the cabin. One thing he spotted right off was the notched boot. The same man who'd been in on the killings at the Blake place had been here. That boot would make finding the man easy. The notch was deep enough that it would show when a man stood. Rafferty stepped to his horse, but staggered when he raised a leg to mount.

He realized he was desperately thirsty. The blood loss from the head wound probably had contributed to that. He walked the horse over to the well and used a bucket to haul up some water. It was good and cold. He drank deeply, and afterwards he gave some to the horse. He dipped his bandana in the water and dabbed at the caked blood on the side of his head. He gritted his teeth at the stinging, but continued to clean out the wound.

Suddenly, the earth seemed to heave. At first Rafferty thought it was a reaction to the pain, but then he saw the horse rear in surprise and fear. He tried to hold on to the well wall, but it, too, was shaking.

It was an earthquake, the first Rafferty had experienced in this country, although he'd heard they weren't uncommon. It knocked him to his knees, and when he tried to stand back up, a shot of pain went through him. Rafferty passed out and fell.

It was dark when he woke, lying in a heap next to the well, with the horse standing over him. The stars told him it was near dawn, but it was a good hour before light. His head felt clearer, but there'd be no trailing the kidnappers in this darkness. He pulled the saddle gear off the horse and got it a bait of corn before letting it into the paddock. With a bucket of water, he went to the cabin to tend to the wound. He had a small mirror there, and he worked by the light of a lantern at cleaning up the blood and inspecting the holes. The slug had given him a good blow on the skull and something of a concussion, but the wounds looked pretty clean. He was lucky. An inch to the side and he'd be a dead man, as Kern and the other thought he was. He'd just finished, and had wrapped the head in a clean bandana when something caught his attention.

There was a sound, a scratching sound, from the outside corner of the cabin. Rafferty doused the lantern and drew his sidearm. He stood up slowly, but there was none of the faint-headedness that had caused him to lose consciousness earlier. That, at least, seemed to indicate improvement.

He heard the sound again, and it occurred to him it didn't sound like a man walking or sneaking up on the place.

It was something else.

He thought of the dog.

'Wolf?'

There was a low answering whine, and Rafferty was out the door to the corner. The coming dawn had lighted the eastern sky sufficiently that Rafferty could see dimly.

His big dog lay on its belly, shot but alive. The beast's right shoulder was a mass of caked blood and dirt, and there appeared to be another wound across the hips. Rafferty could see the dog had dragged itself twenty or thirty yards across the clearing to reach the cabin. A trail of blood marked the path. He figured that the dog had attacked the kidnappers and been shot by one of them.

He carried the big canine onto the low porch and set about cleaning its wounds. The shoulder wound was a deep one, and it was right at the joint. The joint seemed chipped, but there didn't look like there were any other broken bones there.

The other slug had entered the dog's back, two-thirds of the distance down from the shoulders. It had nicked the spine and gone on down through some leg muscle. As Rafferty felt around the dog's right leg, he found the hard lump of the slug, just below the hide. He pulled out his knife and made a small slice above the slug. It popped out easily.

It was clear the dog's hind quarters were paralyzed, but Rafferty had no way of knowing whether that would be per-manent. He'd known of men who'd come back from paralysis a few days or weeks after that kind of a wound. Wolf was a good dog, a strong one, and if there was a chance, Rafferty figured the animal would make it.

When he'd cleaned the wounds up the best he could, Rafferty got a horse blanket and carefully laid the dog on it, in front of the cabin where the animal could see things, but sheltered from the elements. Baker had left some antelope hanging, and Rafferty cut off a big hunk of it for the dog. He chopped it into bite-size pieces so Wolf wouldn't strain the wounds pulling and tearing at the meat. He set a pot of water next to the animal's bed.

'I'll get 'em for you, fella. I know you done your best, and I'll take over from here,' Rafferty spoke to the dog, one hand cradling the big snout and the other stroking the animal's head.

It was light enough to see now, and in minutes, Rafferty was mounted. But he realized immediately he would not be able to stay in the saddle. There was still too much dizziness. He got down, unsaddled the horse and laid down to rest. Sleep came quickly. When he woke again, the day was gone. There would be no trailing them in the dark, and the night looked clear. If it did not rain, he would still be able to follow their tracks in the morning. He fried up some bacon and chewed on a piece of dried bread. His appetite was back. Three hours later he cooked up a small stew with pieces of meat, some potatoes, wild onions he had planted near the well, and some dried herbs he picked when he found them and kept at the cabin for cooking. He slept once more, waking at his normal time in the pre-dawn hour. In minutes he was dressed, mounted and on the trail. His head hurt, but the dizziness was gone. He felt strong. He felt angry.

How many ways were there for a man to die? How many ways to be shot? How many ways to starve, to wither of lack of water, to die of disease, to break limbs and tear organs and die a painful, shuddering death?

How many ways?

Too many, or just enough. That was the way of life. Its living had as many twists and turns as its ending. Hugh Rafferty rode easily, on his way to meet a man who called himself Simon, a name almost certainly not his own. Rafferty smelled his own sweat and that of his horse. He smelled the richness of his saddle leather, felt the stirrups encasing his boots, the pad under his heel, the rawhide lariat that bobbed against his right knee. The reins lay over his palm, he did a quick hitch and they fell between fingers, so he could better control them if he so chose.

Rafferty heard the clop of the horses' hoofs on the trail leading into Springwater. He felt he heard, smelled and saw everything that was to be perceived in these moments. He caught sight of a fieldmouse scampering around the base of a clump of grass, a bird's nest in a mesquite bush, a rattler asleep by a wide rock. None of them marked his passing. He was as one with them, no danger to them. His goal was not more important than theirs, only different.

The trail was not difficult to follow. They'd made no effort to hide the tracks, and they'd put Louise on one of Rafferty's own horses. A man with the old Ranger's skills could have followed any of the horses after having viewed their tracks in the yard next to the cabin, but having one of his own to follow made it even easier. Two hours into the day the sun was not yet over the ridgeline, but Rafferty knew where they held Louise.

It was a shack between his place and the Blake spread. Nothing special, but sufficiently out of the way that no one else would have seen the men escorting the woman, and so the townspeople wouldn't begin talking. Simon had no particular reputation in town, so far. He was a man with some money, who had hired some hands. Rafferty hadn't been talking about the clashes between them, and he was sure Simon hadn't, either. Before he took the battle to them, he would need to let people know what was going on.

There was another small ranch, not much bigger than Blake's place, three miles away. The Andersons were well-respected in town as hard-workers who got in no one's way and who paid their bills. And Hilda Anderson was reputed as the best bear-sign maker in the country. Cowboys would ride from all over and trade for the treats of fried dough. They swapped what they could. Some offered work around the Anderson spread, while others would bring toys they'd carved for the Anderson youngsters. It was a regular stopping-off point, and a good place to drop a piece of information if you wanted it to get around.

Mrs Anderson was standing on her front porch, wiping her hands on her apron when he rode up. She called to her husband, who appeared from their small barn with a pitchfork in his hand.

'Hugh Rafferty, it's been too long,' she said. 'I got some coffee on, but I'm sorry to tell you I haven't made any 'sign today. Got some muffins, though. Light and set.'

The kids were everywhere. The Andersons had five of their own and two others they'd adopted, the kids of families killed by Indians. Rafferty saw a shy girl standing by the corner of the house, staring at him. He winked and she ducked back behind the house. There were a couple of toddlers and an older boy off digging a trench by the barn. When Olaf Anderson had joined them, Rafferty told them the story of the Blakes, the attacks on him and his place, and the kidnapping of Louise Briggs.

'All I'm asking you is to let the word get around, so's people know why I'm moving the way I am,' he said.

'They went after the Blakes, they might come after us next,' Olaf said. 'Maybe I come with you?'

'I appreciate the offer, Olaf, but this is the kind of thing I do. I'm an old Ranger, and I've been with guns and trouble all my life. You, you're the kind of person that's going to build this country, that's going to make something of it, farming, raising families, establishing towns and schools. No, you stay here and do what you do. My kind may be a vanishing breed, but there's still a need for us in these situations. Besides, I'm not entirely alone,' Rafferty said.

The Andersons took a look at his wound and she put a

clean pad on it, but they said it appeared to be clean and starting to heal. She seemed to want to fuss over him, but didn't. A Western woman might want a man to stay away from dangerous situations, might want to protect him from going out where he might get killed, but she knew there were things that needed done, and if they didn't get done, the West would eat them up. It was a country and a kind of people that needed constant attention. Given a chance, it still had the means to revert back to what it was before the first white man set foot here, even in these heady days of railroads and all. Rafferty had work to do, and these people knew it. He rode off within a half hour of his arrival, heading back for the shack and Louise.

CHAPTER TWENTY-ONE

There were three of them who'd taken her. The man with the notched heel and two others. It was likely they'd been told he'd been shot before they went to the cabin for her. He couldn't imagine why they'd taken her, unless it was just to get the RS Connected vacated. They must not have found out that Baker was with the ranch. Unless they'd been keeping a careful watch on the place and had seen his fairly infrequent visits, there'd be no way to tell. Baker looked like what he claimed to be, an itinerant gold-seeker. He didn't sleep at the cabin, so a watcher might come to the conclusion he was an outsider even if the visits had been noted. It was likely they'd failed altogether to include Baker in the formula. That would be a mistake, because if everything else went their way, they'd still have a hard time overcoming a determined Quanah Baker.

Rafferty considered the terrain as he approached the shack where he figured Louise was being held. It was in a low, grassy spot, overhung by a couple of big old pines. The structure was just an old eight-foot by fourteen-foot, shed-roofed shack with a dirt floor. He recalled a rude fireplace to one side, more than you'd expect for just a line cabin. Somebody before the Blakes came along had spent some

117

time living here. There were nice carved hooks along the walls for hats and coats, and the bench out front showed signs of having had some time spent sitting on it. There was enough grass around to picket horses right alongside the shack.

The place was in broken country, which was both good and bad for Rafferty. It would be easy, if they had any kind of a lookout, for them to see him coming over a rise. He kept to the low places and avoided skylining himself as he approached. The benefit was that if he remained unnoticed from afar, he could get up to them, getting good and close before they spotted him.

He dismounted a half mile from the shack. He'd picked up the trail again, and as he'd suspected, it was leading directly for the shack. Rafferty pulled off his boots and slipped on the moccasins Louise had made. He checked his pistol and the spare shells on his gunbelt, giving each of them a little spin to be sure they'd come out easily when he needed to reload. Then he turned his attention to the rifle. It was fully loaded and he had a pocketful of extra rounds. He took a second pistol and slipped it into his belt. His hat caused him discomfort as it sat over the swelling of his head wounds. It didn't bother him much riding, but he wanted to be sure it would not distract him. He left it with the horse and started out at an easy jog that took him within 200 yards of the shack. His head hurt with each footfall, but it wasn't serious, and he was able to keep his attention on the work at hand. He still hadn't seen the shack, having stayed out of sight of its occupants, but he knew this country, and he had two low rises to cross. He walked and then crawled to the lowest spot in the first rise, saw no one, and rolled over the edge to the swale ahead. He'd have the structure in sight over the next rise, and he picked his spot carefully.

There was a low bush on one side of the summit. He worked his way up to the bush, and raised his head directly behind it to get a rough picture. It was fifty yards to the cabin, and only one man was in sight. Three horses were picketed just up the rise from the shack. One was the horse Louise had been riding. That meant one of the kidnappers was missing. Was he reporting in somewhere or scouting around? If the latter, had he crossed Rafferty's trail and found the horse? There was no time to worry about it. Rafferty had to locate the second man at the shack and find out where Louise was.

They'd shot the dog, and that gave him the idea. Perhaps these men had heard the wolf stories he'd told the ones who'd tracked him out of town. Rafferty cupped his hands and gave a low howl.

The man sitting on a bench out front of the cabin jerked to his feet, rifle in his hands, and looked for the source of the sound. He had bandages made of bandanas wrapped around his upper thigh and around his right forearm. This, then, was the man Wolf had attacked. Rafferty turned his cupped hands to the right and howled again. The move threw the sound in that direction, and the man turned away from Rafferty to try to spot whatever might be there. Rafferty heard him swear, and the rickety door swung open.

A second man stood there, holding Louise in front of him. She was tied hand and foot. Rafferty howled again, and they all looked off to his right. The ranger turned to his left and threw a lower-pitched howl. He lay on his belly, and cradled the rifle easily on sturdy triangles formed by his arms and elbows. As the men looked back and forth he saw Louise suddenly look right at him and nod.

Rafferty laid the rifle sights precisely between her breasts and waited. She winked again, and dropped suddenly to the ground. The man who'd been standing behind her was a perfect target as Rafferty pulled the trigger. The man was thrown back into the doorway. Rafferty rolled over twice, then took a breath to ease the spinning in his head. The second man had his rifle up. He searched the horizon and found his spot, aiming for the puff of gunpowder smoke from Rafferty's rifle. The man fired, but Rafferty lay six feet away. The gunman got a second shot off before the former Ranger's first slug took him in the head. It was over in seconds. Louise motioned with her head that it was safe to approach, and Rafferty quickly jogged to the shack to cut her free.

'They figured you were dead, Hugh.'

'Close. It was a near thing.'

'I figured you were harder than that to kill. I knew that howling had to be one of you, and I didn't expect Quanah would have gotten back to the cabin yet, so I knew it had to be you out there.'

'It's good to know you keep your wits about you.'

'I'm a Briggs, Rafferty, and don't you forget it. Did you bring me a gun?'

Rafferty handed her his waist gun.

'Where's the third one?' he said.

'He's been going out every couple of hours for an inspection tour. I expect he heard the shooting. He should be back soon,' she said.

A voice spoke behind them.

'Sooner than you thought.'

Rafferty held his hands away from his pistol. He'd laid down the rifle when he cut Louise free.

'Mind if I turn around?' he said.

'Your funeral. You can look it in the face,' the man said.

Rafferty turned, taking a step away from Louise as he did so. He noticed she'd hidden her pistol in the folds of her skirt.

He looked at the gunman, standing alongside his horse. He'd walked up through the grass while Rafferty was cutting Louise free, and both had been so preoccupied they'd not noticed him. But Rafferty noticed him now, with his red shirt and his pistol in his fist.

'I know you,' Rafferty said. 'I didn't know these boys here, but I know you.'

'What of it?'

'You're Jack Henry.'

The man looked surprised.

'You're a no good drygulcher and a killer of women.'

'What are you talking about?'

'Your boys back at the saloon aren't going to be too worried about the fact that you and your buddy came after me. Lying in wait for a man is bad, but it just makes you a common outlaw, no better than a horse thief.

'But killing women is different. Maybe you didn't think about it. Maybe you figured nobody would find out. But they will. When the boys back at the saloon find out you killed Mrs Blake, a friendly woman who never hurt a soul, that's going to look bad. And when we add the fact that you kidnapped Miss Briggs here, well – Western communities don't think much of men who mistreat women, Henry, they surely don't.'

'I don't know what you're talking about. I never had anything to do with the Blakes.'

'That makes you a liar to boot. There's evidence, Henry, hard evidence. I left the mark on you myself back there when I shot at you and your friend in brown, the one I killed. When you boys came galloping out of that gully meaning to kill me, I dusted you with a slug, but it caught the heel of your boot. I can see the gash from here, and you've left the print everywhere you've gone. A tenderfoot could follow your trail. It's as good as leaving a card with your name on it. The notched heel identifies you, Jack Henry, as the worst kind of scum in the West.'

Jack Henry was nervous, and he was angry. He knew the truth in what Rafferty was saying, but he also knew the solution.

'Rafferty, you're a dead man in any case. I met with one of the boys out there. Sent him back to town with the word that you ain't dead. Means they'll have a killing party on the road in minutes. They've had enough of you, Rafferty. It's over, trying to scare you off. The man put the word out. There's two hundred in gold for the man that kills you.

'And there's the other thing. They say Big Jim Dunedin is heading this way. You might hold off all the rest of us, but nobody stops Big Jim Dunedin. It just ain't done. He's comin' here, and he's comin' mad. I guess you know why.

'But I don't figure to wait for Dunedin, and I don't figure to wait for the rest of the boys. You see, Rafferty, you can say anything you want about me here. It won't matter. I figure to collect that two hundred myself. The talk, anything I did, it won't matter if I kill you – both of you – right here,' he said.

His eyes were on Rafferty's.

'I'm going to give you a chance. Draw, Rafferty.'

Rafferty was ready to risk it. He'd draw and step to the left, another step away from Louise, and he'd risk catching some lead. He began his move, saw Henry squeeze his pistol, heard a boom, and then a second. And before he could get his own gun into firing position, he watched Jack Henry crumple with a shot through his shirt pocket.

He hadn't fired a shot, and the man was dead. He smelled the burnt gunpowder from the pistol in Louise Briggs' small fist. She stood, feet apart, steady, a little wide-eyed, but confident. Henry lay twitching on the ground. She kept her attention on him until it was clear he was done moving around. Rafferty dropped his handgun back into its holster.

'I think you shoot better than your father did, Louise.'

'Had to,' she said. 'If there's one thing he taught me, it's that, when you've got it to do, you've got to do it. We've got some shooting left to do. I couldn't have you killed in cold blood,' she said, stuffing the smoking pistol into the belt of her skirt.

She looked at the bandage on his head.

'You break open that head wound?'

'Not the one you know about. Got shot again. That's what kept me.'

'You want me to look at it?'

'Naw. Mrs Anderson took care of it. It's fine.'

'Lucky you've got a skull made of oak. One of these days, they're going to learn not to shoot for your head, Hugh Rafferty, and then you might be in trouble. Let's ride.'

Rafferty had figured out there was no way he was going to keep Louise Briggs from riding along. Now he was thinking hard how to keep her out of the fighting to come. She'd asked for spare shells as soon as they'd ridden out, reloading the pistol as they rode and dropping the remaining shells into a pocket in her skirt.

'They came up all of a sudden. I was kneading some bread and singing to myself, like a fool, and I didn't realize they were there until they were standing at the door. First thing I heard, Wolf was on that one guy's leg. Name of Calder. Tore a good chunk out of him, and when the man tried to beat him away, Wolf grabbed his forearm and worked on that some. Henry there, he was pretty good with a gun. He put one hole in Wolf that knocked him down, then Calder pulled his gun and shot him again. I figured he was dead. I've got to tell you, forget what they did to me. I wanted those men dead for what they did to the dog,' she said.

'Wolf and me, we don't kill very easy. The old boy's in real bad shape, but I think he'll make it. I left him out front, guarding the place until we get back. What happened then?'

'Well, they grabbed at me, and I went after them with my rolling pin. Damn! I could kick myself for not having my pistol with me. I tussled with Henry and the other one, and finally they held me down. They called Calder, bleeding as he was, to come tie me while they held me.'

'So it was his blood on the floor. I was afraid it was yours.'

'I came out of it pretty well after all. That Jack Henry, he tried to start something while I was tied up. If you were to go back and look at the body, you might find a nice set of tooth prints in his shoulder. I yelled good and loud, and the others showed up right quick. Henry was bad, but he didn't want the other two to think he'd take advantage of a woman tied up. He stayed away after that.'

Rafferty asked her what she'd learned from the kidnappers.

'It turns out this Simon is a real slick fellow. He's staying in the background and letting Kern do all his hiring and firing. Everybody knows Simon is the boss, but nobody talks to him about the business they're doing but Kern. And they hardly ever see him except when he comes over to the saloon and works with cards. He's smooth, the boys said. Can deal tops, bottoms, seconds, like he was born to it,' Louise said.

'Did any of them say anything about his background? Anybody know where he came from?'

'That's the strange thing. They don't know. Nobody'd ever heard of Simon before, and nobody's seen him before. But from what they say, he sometimes uses river terminology, so they figured maybe he was a big man on the riverboats, got run off or something. Or came up with a big pot and headed out. He's paying those boys in gold.'

'He'll need plenty of gold to keep them if he figures to run the RS Connected. There's no big money in this range.'

'That's another thing. The boys are starting to ask questions. Couple of them have just ridden off, they said. They included a bunch that you ran off just before all this happened. They don't figure there's much gold. They were saying that's just a story Simon conjured up to keep them interested when the going got tough. Now, some of them are saying fighting wages aren't enough when you're up against a man like Rafferty, and ghost wolves and whatever else is in those hills. They're some spooked, Hugh.'

'Spooky country, and I like it that way. Enhance it when I can. Keeps people from wandering too freely where they don't belong. But if his men are on to him, Simon's at his most dangerous. He'll have to finish the job in a hurry to keep from losing his edge. The edge is the men with him. He won't want them thinking twice, or he'll have them slipping away in the middle of a gunfight, when he needs to be able to count on them.'

CHAPTER
TWENTY-TWO

As they rode along, Louise asked, 'What was that Henry was saying about the man Dunedin?'

Rafferty was quiet a moment before responding.

'That has me more worried that anything else. I know Big Jim Dunedin, and I don't want to cross him. If there's a man alive I don't want to cross, it's him.'

'Why,' she said.

'It goes back to my Ranger days. Turns out three of us Rangers came riding into town just a few minutes after a bank robbery had been tried, and I ended up chasing one of them boys. There were four of them in the gang that hit the bank. A downstreet lookout, a man to hold the horses and two to go inside the bank. It was pretty well thought out, but they didn't count on the folks in that town.

'That town like every town in the west was full of hard cases. They'd been carrying guns all their lives, and this was before folks started suggesting you leave your guns at home when you walked the streets of a town.

'Well, it turned out the banker had a gun in his desk. They winged him, but he killed one of the robbers right there on the bank floor. That set the town on notice, and the fellow holding the horses, well, he got it next. He had his gun out and was looking up and down for trouble. The storekeeper came out from across the street, and that man with the horses made the mistake of pointing the gun his way. Storekeeper'd picked up his old Sharps from behind the door when he stepped out, and he just fired from the hip. Knocked himself back into the store, the kick of that rifle, but it blew a hole in that bandit that he just naturally couldn't deal with. That was two dead. The second of the two who'd gone into the bank, he lit out of there like a shot, cut around behind the bank to get off the main street and stole the first horse he found.

'A couple of cowboys and the saloonkeeper stepped into the saddles and had him run down within a mile. In his hurry, the robber had picked a sorry old mare that just wasn't up to the chase. He pulled a gun on those boys, and that was that. There were three holes in him, and each of the three men in that posse claimed his was the killing shot.

'Now, nobody'd noticed the boy acting as lookout at the end of the town until it was over. That was a young gunhand named Johnny Dunedin. The townsfolk started backtracking the three bandits and found there'd been four. They found where he'd been standing during the robbery and they were just about to head after him when the three of us Rangers rode in.

'Now, we had other business, but we drew straws and I got the short one. They went on and left me to go after young Dunedin, bring him to justice.

'Them townsfolk, they wanted that boy, bad. It was just a black mark, the way they figured, that anybody'd even think of coming after their bank. The fact that three of the four were dead and not a penny had been taken didn't faze them a bit. But I pointed out that this boy looked to have a good horse, from what people remembered, and from the look of his tracks. I said they probably had fresh mounts off down the trail some, and now this boy would have his choice of them. It likely would be a long chase, and he already had three or four hours of lead. Well, the townspeople still wanted him, but they allowed as to how they had ranches and businesses to run and couldn't spare a week or two chasing a boy across this country. So they decided to let me do it.

'I said he was a boy. That's what a couple of folks remembered. You know small Western towns. Nobody comes into town without everybody coming to take a look, and when four of them came in, people naturally came to their windows to read the sign.

'He'd tried to stay mostly out of sight, out by a big tree at one end of town. Figured he was supposed to whistle or fire a shot if anybody came riding in. Never got the chance.

'I took out after him, but that boy was pretty good. He had four horses stashed like I'd figured. He set two of them free and must have fired a shot or something, because they took off at a gallop. Did that so nobody following him could use them. Then he switched his saddle to one of the other two and headed out, with those two spare horses. He switched horses regularly all that day, and I knew I wasn't gaining on him. I had one spare horse of my own, and I was treating my mounts well, knowing it looked like a long one.

'He tried all the regular tricks. In one stream bed, I kept on him by watching for rocks overturned by his horses, and in another I could pick out the general pattern of a rougher bottom on the side he'd gone up. Not enough to trail him, but enough to tell me which way he'd gone. Then it was only a question of looking for the place where he left the water, and that was easily found. He cut across rocky places, he even tried dragging some branches behind his horses to wipe the tracks out.

'Where he could, that boy'd take off down an established trail to try and get his tracks mixed with the others. But one of his horses had a cracked shoe, and it was pretty simple following that. I could pick it out and keep moving at a good clip. That horse came up lame in that leg on the third day, and he cut it loose. It made the tracking a little tougher, but then he was down to two horses, same as me, and I was willing to spend the time keeping on him.

'I learned a few things about the boy on the trail. Picked up fibres from a branch he brushed against, showed me he was still wearing the blue shirt they'd seen him wearing in town. I found places where he'd camped and where his horses had rolled, and I knew he had a paint and a dun, and the paint was the better horse. Hell, I knew what he ate, which side he rolled out of his bedding, how he got his horses ready in the morning.

'After a week of tracking a man, you get so you think like him. Have to, if you're going to stay on his trail. I had the townspeople's description, but by the end of a week, I could have described him as well, and could tell you about his habits.

'He was pretty well trained for a youngster, but he didn't have the fine points that makes an expert on the trail. I'd come across Indian boys better at leaving no sign.

'Well, on the tenth day, the boy came across another rider. It was all there, plain as the writing in a book. We'd been heading northwest, and I was just a couple of hours behind him. The other horse had come up from the south. They'd talked a few minutes, you could see the milling of the horses in the dust. Then the horse from the south continued on across the trail and headed on, keeping in the same direction he'd been going. The boy kept on, and I stayed with him.

'I should have gotten suspicious. The next two nights' camps, there was no sign left except for the fire. It occurred to me later that all the footprints had been swept away, or he'd stepped on stones so as not to leave any. I didn't worry, because I'd seen the boy's prints before, and

I knew I'd recognize them.

'On the third day after the other rider had crossed the trail, everything disappeared. That boy's trail just plain vanished. There was nothing.

'Well, I backtracked and came up again, and there it was, gone. So I started a crossing pattern, spreading wider and wider, to try to pick something up. I found it. He'd gotten to a rocky area, covered the horses' hoofs and backtracked a quarter mile, then he'd taken off in a different direction.

'I was back on the trail, but that set me to thinking. Where'd this boy suddenly come up with a trick like that?

'The trail was gone once more, and I found it. Then there was a place he'd cut up into a little canyon and come up the back to a bluff. It was an hour's ride up the canyon, and he'd cut back out to the cliff overlooking the canyon mouth, and he'd watched me as I went in. Could have picked me off, but he didn't. It made me shiver later, when I saw how that man could shoot.

'It was when I'd gotten to the top of that bluff myself and seen what he'd done that I knew they'd tricked me.

'I was following the same two horses, but I wasn't following the same man!

'Once I knew that, it wasn't hard to figure what'd happened. There was only one possible place, and that was where that horse had crossed from south to north. The riders had swapped horses without getting down. Must have just hopped from horse to horse, with the boy heading north on the trail the other man had taken, using his horse, while the other traveller had taken the paint and dun.

'I knew what had happened, but I didn't know why, and I was right puzzled.

'I got down in the shade of an old lightning-struck pine, built myself a little fire and cooked up some coffee. I drank it, chewed some jerky and sat and thought it out for a while. I'd lost the boy for sure now, I'd been nearly three days heading north-west, and if that boy was smart, he'd have swung around and headed south-east, so he could be six, seven days away, depending on his horse and how much time he'd spent covering his tracks.

'I figured I might as well keep on the trail of his horses, and see if I could get some answers.

'I knew what had happened, but I was just plain stumped about the why of it. What could that boy have said that'd convince some stranger to swap horses, and head out, covering his tracks, obviously knowing he was being follows. It made no sense.

'I finished the coffee and got back on the trail.

'That man was the best Injun I ever followed. He knew every trick I'd ever heard of, and taught me a couple of others. But I'd had some good teachers. He could slow me down, but he couldn't lose me. That, and my horses were better than his. He tried it all, but we just kept comin', and I was closing.

'It was two full weeks from the bank robbery when I finally got him within rifle range, although if I'd been riding his horses and he mine, he'd have been gone. The paint and dun were tired horses, I could see it in their gait on the trail, and when I spotted them, I could see they didn't have a lot left.

'The rider was good, and he was giving those horses every break he could, without actually giving up the chase. He was a man who appreciated horses, and I could sense that he didn't like pushing them this hard.

'Finally we came off a hillside into a valley of low brush and grass, and I decided to take it to him. I was on a long-legged black that purely did love to run and, although he was tired, when I asked him, he jumped and started running that man down. In those days I carried a good old handgun, a Smith & Wesson .32 six-shooter. But for this, although I didn't figure to shoot the man if I could help it,

I got my long gun out. It was a good one, too. One of Chris Spencer's seven-shot repeaters. Well, that black had some bottom and I let my other horse go, figuring to come back for him later. It was clear this race wasn't going to last a mile. That man's mounts were dead beat, but they were game. He was on the dun, but he pulled the paint up along-side and swung over to ride that horse bareback. He had his rifle in one hand and the reins in the other, and it was a thing to see. A real piece of horsemanship. The dun just stopped cold on the trail when he let her go. She had nothing left.

'Well, the paint kind of stumbled up around a patch of brush, but the man stayed up, and swung the horse, and was back into a full gallop. The man looked back and I can remember my surprise. He had his reins in his teeth, with his rifle in one hand and his pistol in the other. For a minute there I was glad it was me chasing him instead of him chasing me.

'I was only fifty yards back and going all out, and when I came to the place where he'd stumbled, I saw too late why it was. There was a big hole in the ground there, like an underground cavern that had its roof caved in. Last thing I remember was the black rearing up to miss it and then both of us falling into the blackness.

'I woke up with my leg broke. The black was dead with a busted neck. It was a fine mess I was in. This cave was, oh, fifteen feet deep and wider at the bottom than the top, so there was no way to climb out, even if I'd had two legs to climb with.

'That man I was chasing, he came right back, dropped a rope and used his horse to haul me out. Then he set up a camp next to some grass, caught up the horses and picketed them on the grass. He patched me up and put a splint on that leg. He left me there and went out hunting. He brought in a deer and a couple of turkeys, and we spent two weeks in that camp.

'Big Jim Dunedin was his name. He was a mountain man, got his wilderness training trapping for furs and trading with Indians. The boy who'd been lookout at that bank job was his younger brother, Johnny. He'd been tracking Johnny after hearing the boy had fallen into bad company. He'd come into the town a day after the bank job, had a hunch where Johnny would go, and cut straight there. Said he'd spent a whole day alongside both of us before he arranged the meeting on the trail. He'd told Johnny to take his horse and told him where to head, and then he took over leading me down the path.

'Young Johnny Dunedin had been in with some bad ones, but the bank job was his first known criminal act, and he hadn't taken an active part. Big Jim argued for the boy. He said the banker had only been winged and was back at work the day after the robbery attempt, so the boy wasn't responsible for any murders. He said he wanted, as a matter of family pride, to steer the boy right. He asked me to drop the chase.

'Well, I had this broke leg, and he wasn't about to tell me where the boy had gone, so I said, as long as that boy doesn't get his name connected with anything else, I was willing to drop it.

'Big Jim got me well enough to ride, and then set me on my way.'

Rafferty stopped his horse to continue the story.

'Big Jim Dunedin had done me a big favour, and I'd done him a small one, and it seemed like we parted on good terms.

'I wasn't exactly scared of the man, but I sure didn't look forward to bracing him. Big Jim Dunedin sized up as the most self-assured, competent man I'd ever come across. Back then he carried an old 50-calibre Sharps. He said he'd converted the old breech-loader to handle cartridges, and old Christian Sharps couldn't have done a better job. He talked fondly of an old, ten-pound Hawken he'd traded off Jim Bridger. Apparently he'd had to trade that to some Indians one time, traded for his hide. Later he ended up with the Sharps. He was as good a rifle shot as I've seen, and he could handle short guns and knives as if he'd been born with them. He carried a matched pair of '51 single action Navy Colts, six-shooters. I was glad he hadn't hung out with a bad crowd as a youngster, because he'd have taken a few Rangers with him, I can tell you.

'I figured that if anybody had a chance of turning Johnny Dunedin straight, it'd be Big Jim. They were a good fifteen years apart, and Big Jim had left the family homestead by the time Johnny was born. The boy'd been raised without a father, and Big Jim kinda felt responsible for his turning bad.

'Well, I figured he talked some sense to that boy. I never heard from Johnny Dunedin again. Not until six months ago.'

'What happened?' Louise said.

'I killed him. He came here after me, he pulled a gun on me, and I killed him.'

CHAPTER
TWENTY-THREE

Neither of them spoke for a time, then Louise, trying to lighten the mood, talked of something she'd heard on the stage into Springwater.

'I heard of a bank robbery that reminded me of that one you mentioned with Dunedin and the others. Up in Northfield, Minnesota. The way I heard it, the Jameses and the Youngers, and three other men got together and figured to make one big one before they got out of the area. It was getting too hot back there, and the Jameses, they both had wives to worry about. Well, they hit this bank in Northfield, and every single thing went wrong. They couldn't get the tellers to open the safe. The townfolks got a warning, and they just came out with their guns. They chased that band of bandits right out of town. Killed two of them and wounded one of the Youngers. Two of the Youngers left town riding double.

'I heard in the old days, the ones that ran might have made a clean getaway, but you can't outrun the telegraph. Two weeks later, a posse killed another man and captured all three Youngers. I hear they're ready to plead guilty so they don't hang. Jesse and Frank, well, they just disappeared. Could be right around here, for all I know.'

Rafferty was quiet for a moment, as if considering the possibility. He shook his head.

'Sounds like those boys might finally have learned their lesson. They'd likely fight shy of a deal like this, and leave the country if one started up,' he said.

They walked their horses easily. There was no big hurry, just a job that needed doing when Rafferty got to Springwater. He cast about with his eyes as they rode, watching for sign. A mile from the line shack, he pulled up, worried anyway, and what he saw added to it.

'We've got trouble,' he said, pointing to hoofprints in a section of hard-packed dirt. The tracks were both coming and going, and they had been made by the same horse.

'Yes. I noticed the tracks, too. Doesn't look like any of the horses those three rode.'

They backtracked and found a spot where the horse had stopped, and then turned and headed back toward the town.

'Somebody come from Springwater to talk to them boys. Could be Henry was telling the truth about having warned somebody,' Rafferty said.

'That's how I see it. The tracks are fresh, so he must have cut and run when he heard the shots. Even if Henry didn't warn him, he might have cut your trail, Hugh, which means they'll have a welcome party waiting. Maybe we should collect Quanah before we move in.'

'This business can't wait. The more time we give them now, the slimmer our chances. I'm going to have to do the best I can.'

'We'll do the best we can, Hugh.'

He turned in the saddle. The wind caught her hair, and the overall picture she made conveyed a sense of fragility and beauty. But her face was stern and her eyes hard. He couldn't let her be involved, but she wouldn't be left out.

'Women don't fight gunfights, Louise. It's just not done.'

She looked at him long and hard, and then shook her head.

'Hugh Rafferty, you're making no sense.'

'I'm serious.'

'Think about what you're saying! Women have been fighting with guns in this country since the very first. They have stood by their men and children, loading guns and firing them to protect them from Indians and bears and outlaws. There are stories about women who stood over their wounded husbands and fought off the enemy when their men couldn't fight no longer. Women taking up guns to protect what's theirs is nothing new in the West.'

'But Louise. This isn't your fight. You don't have to be here, and you have no business risking yourself on my behalf.'

She reached across the space between them and pulled on his reins, hauling both horses to a stop.

'Hugh Rafferty, you're a thick-headed old fool, but I didn't think you were that thick-headed. I was hoping for a different place and time to talk about this, but it looks like this will have to do.

'I'm not here to be a houseguest. I'm not here to be a daughter to you. I can't imagine how you've missed it, but in case you haven't noticed, I'm in love with you. I want to marry you and I want to populate the RS Connected with Rafferty kids, every one of whom will have Briggs for a middle name. That's why I'm here. I've loved you since I was a child, and now I'm old enough to do something about it.'

He sat still, as surprised as if he'd been doused with a bucket of cold water, but realizing what she said was what he himself wanted.

'Well?' she said.

'I'm too old . . . I'm old enough to be your . . . .'

'Father? You're full of beans, Rafferty. You'd have had to have started pretty young to arrange that, and even if you were old enough, it would make no difference. You were plenty younger than Jim Briggs.'

'What would he think. . . .'

'I've got you there, too, Rafferty. Before he died, he gave us his blessing. Said he'd always hoped for it, if you ever found a place to settle down. He said it'd take a man as strong as you to handle a woman like me. I agreed with him. It was a dying man's wish, Rafferty. You can't deny that, unless, well . . . .' Her voice caught.

'Unless what?'

'Unless you don't love me, Hugh. Unless you want to send me away.'

Thoughts roiled about in his head. Two emotions fought within him, his need for this woman, and his need to protect her from harm. It came to him that there was one way, as much as it would hurt, to protect her from the gun-fighting to come. He dropped his head, regretting the need to do it, and spoke.

'That's it, Louise. I love you like a daughter, not as a man should love a woman.' His discomfort was real, talking about such things. 'Um, maybe it would be easier if you just rode on. . . .'

There was a fire in her eyes. Her cheekbones blazed red.

'You bastard! I know what you're doing! Well, listen here. I've known you a good many years, and I know a lie when I hear one. I'm going down there with you, and a Briggs gun will kick alongside a Rafferty gun, just as they have before, whether you want me or not. I owe that to my dad. You owe it to him not to deny me that. And that has nothing to do with how I feel about you.'

'You can't, Louise. You just can't.'

'Ride, Rafferty. Let's get this over with.'

There was no more speaking between them. Rafferty

138

detected her sense of anger and hurt. They rode thirty feet apart, she having fallen back.

CHAPTER TWENTY-FOUR

They came up on the riders a mile outside of town, and Rafferty cursed himself for not having kept a better watch.

He turned in the saddle to warn Louise, but when he looked, she was gone. That was good, then. He wondered about her, but he'd face these guns alone, without having to worry that one of them would hurt the woman. It occurred to him he was also relieved they wouldn't be able to accuse him of hiding behind a woman's skirts.

Kern headed the bunch. It was him and five other riders – all hard-bitten gunmen, from the looks of them. Mean men, with tied down guns and dour expressions. Trick wolf howls wouldn't scare them. They were professional killers. Rafferty knew the kind. There was nothing but to face them, and to try to keep them bunched. That way he'd have a chance at getting several of them. The odds were heavily against his surviving this round, and if he did, there was still Simon to deal with.

'This is it, Rafferty,' Kern said. 'You should have gotten out when you could have.'

'I'd like to say the same thing to you, Kern. Matter of fact, I'll still give you a chance to ride out of this country. Just pack up right now and go. Don't bother going back to try to pick up your pay. I'm going after Simon next. You fellows have been riding roughshod over this country too long.'

As he spoke, Rafferty saw a cloud of dust moving in the distance, coming from Springwater. Riders, moving fast, coming this way. Were they more of Simon's men? Kern didn't look like he figured he'd need more. These men with him were, from the look of them, the toughest he'd have. Who, then, were the riders? They'd be here in minutes.

Rafferty decided to chance it, and keep talking. At least the riders would distract the gunmen. That would help, even if they weren't going to take sides.

'Yep,' he said. 'You pushed pretty hard, but you came up empty at every turn. I never had bushwhackers after me so often when I was with the Rangers. Funny, though, they never were good enough. What do you suppose that means, Kern? Boys?

'Unlucky, if you ask me. This whole business is just unlucky. Don't make sense, neither. There's not enough grass in that country to hold enough beef to feed all you fellers, much less make money. And there's no gold there to speak of, you must know that by now. So, what's the story?'

Kern smiled.

'Reckon it's safe to tell you now, Rafferty, being as you won't be repeating it nor living long enough to do anything about it. These boys know, because they been in on it from the first.

'That ranch of yours sure enough is useless for running cows in any numbers worth worrying about. And the gold, well, there's a little colour in a couple of places, but we knew there wasn't much else. What there is, is a trail out of one of those back canyons, that nobody knows about. Simon heard about it from an old mountain man he took some money from in a poker game. That man bet every last thing he had, and finally, he bet information. Described the place generally, and suggested its use. He learned about it from the Indians in these parts. Simon dealt him three kings, and dealt himself a full house, deuces and treys, he says. The man told him where to find this place. Later, he learned Simon had cheated and came after him. He died gutshot. Simon carries a sleeve gun.'

'What's this got to do with why Simon wants the RS Connected?'

'Well, that trail, as a back entrance, and the way your ranch is protected at the mouth of the canyon, makes it just a fine little place for outlaws like these boys here to call home. We've got a little landslide planned. Take hardly any explosive to block the entrance to the ranch, and then there'd be just that one secret way in and out, and you can't get there from Springwater. Like Jackson's Hole or some of the others. And the thing is, there's plenty of pickings within riding distance of the top of the canyon back there: stage routes, towns with payrolls, rich ranches. Simon figures to be the boss man of a right comfortable operation.'

To Rafferty, it sounded like fiction. If there were such a trail, he'd surely know of it. It seemed too elaborate to be true.

The riders coming from town were drawing closer.

'Nice of you to tell me that, Kern, but I'll still ask you to leave the country.'

'Hah! You've got a sense of humour, Rafferty. Let's see if you can keep it when you're dyin'.'

'Look behind you boys. Before you do anything else, better look behind you.'

For a moment, none of them did. It was an old trick, but one of the gunmen finally looked, and swore. In seconds, the others heard the hoofs and also turned. Rafferty casually drew his pistol and brought his rifle up in the other hand.

The riders were led by Olaf Anderson, and they consisted

of the shopkeeper, a half-dozen small ranchers from the area and the notary, who ran a small newspaper on the side. Anderson carried a big shotgun. The notary/newspaper publisher carried an old Sharps .50 that had seen better days. Others had a smattering of rifles and pistols, but every gun was out and pointed at the outlaws.

'Looks to me like I just came up with a full house to beat your three kings, Kern. You still want to try it?'

'Naw, I guess we'll fold and go back to town.'

The shopkeeper spoke up.

'We don't want you boys in town no more. Just ride out out. We don't want to see ya. This town is trying its damnedest to grow into something, and your kind don't help us none.'

One of the outlaws started to protest, but took another look at the array of weaponry and thought better of it. The local men were not gunmen, but they had the edge, and every man in the west in these times could be expected to have experience with weapons and with killing. They'd all been through plenty.

The five were ready to ride away, but Kern, normally pretty cool, was mad.

'Let these boys wonder, Rafferty, but I don't think you can handle me by yourself. You take some killin', but I think I'm the man to do it.'

'You been trying awful hard, Kern. I'll give you a shot. You want to do it standing up or on horseback?'

'Standing up, like a man,' Kern said, making a move as if to get off his horse.

Rafferty, preparing to dismount, dropped the rifle into its scabbard and the pistol into the holster. As he let go of the pistol, he saw Kern go for his own gun.

Desperately, Rafferty grabbed iron, but Kern's pistol was already coming up. He saw the blossom of flame, but he heard the crack of another gun first, then a second crack to

143

accompany Kern's shot.

Rafferty's gun was up and ready to fire, but Kern was already falling backward off his horse, a red spot on his forehead. He'd been hit before he fired, and his shot had gone into the air.

Rafferty turned. Louise Briggs was standing by her horse beneath a tree. Her pistol was in her hand, and the smoke from the shot was wafting into the trees.

She climbed on the horse and rode over.

'Wasn't a fair fight. He tried to pull a sneak,' she said.

'Damn all, Louise! He missed with his first shot anyway, and I could handle him.'

'Probably. But he missed because I hit him first. Besides, I couldn't risk it. You've still got a ranch to save.'

CHAPTER TWENTY-FIVE

Rafferty and Louise rode into Springwater to confront Simon, but when they searched the saloon and the rooms the man had occupied, they found nothing. A boy currying a pony out in front of the stables at the end of town volunteered that he'd left town.

'He took out this morning, Mister Rafferty. He took a couple of them hard cases he always had around, and they took right out. Had their saddle-bags full and a couple of pack horses along, so it didn't look like they figured to be coming back.'

'Thanks, boy,' Rafferty.

'I think they run. I think you finally done scared them off, Mister Rafferty, and you, ma'am. That, and them stories about wolves. Those stories true?'

'Those wolves only chase bad men, boy. You could ride out that way any time, but like anything, ride watchful. Any time you head out into the countryside, you should stay watchful, and most of the time you'll see any trouble before it can get to you.'

'I didn't really believe them wolf stories, much,' the boy said.

Louise laughed.

'You can believe. It's just that the wolf of the RS Connected is a two-legged wolf,' she said.

The boy looked from the woman to the man, shook his head and went back to his currying.

Before they left town, the two picked up a side of bacon and some other supplies that would be needed at the ranch. They rode quietly, not talking about what Louise had said was between them, not discussing the way they felt about each other.

'It's over, the fighting, is it, Hugh?' she said. It was a question, but it sounded half like a prayer, something she wanted badly to believe and to be true.

Rafferty paused, took a deep breath and shook his head.

'No. It's hardly over. There's Big Jim left for sure. He won't have run. That man never found anything that could make him back up, and certainly no man that could do it. And then there's Simon.'

'But Simon's gone,' Louise said, her eyes widening when he brought up the man's name.

'Maybe, but I think not. This whole thing has got to be frustrating to Simon. It has to seem so easy to him. Just one man in the way. One bullet can finish it. He's got to make his own try at putting me down, and then he'll have his way. I think maybe he'll go into hiding for a while until our attention is elsewhere, or else he'll try an immediate attack, figuring we've counted on his running.'

They rode through the narrow pass that led onto the RS Connected range. Rafferty noticed again how green the narrow valleys were, full of grass for a few selected head. It was not much range, but what there was, was good. And the place was beautiful. That was one of the things that had attracted him to it. Some folks liked the long, flat plains. Some appreciated that country like the big Llano Estacado of west Texas, whose only features were the buffalo wallows that filled with water in the rainy times and turned into

146

cracked mud-holes in the dry.

Rafferty, well, he liked country with a little vertical defin-ition. Mountain passes and cliffsides. Pines hanging on to a steep talus. He'd found it in the RS Connected, and he meant to keep it.

He snuck a look sideways at Louise Briggs. There was a woman, the kind of woman born to help run a tough range like this. Good with a gun, she rode as if she'd been born on a horse. And there wasn't any room for giving ground in this one. If Rafferty wanted a partner, he couldn't ask for a better one. Trouble was, he'd never figured on a wife up here. He'd sort of planned it out as a solitary pursuit, figur-ing he'd end up an aged, crotchety bachelor mountain man, if he lived that long.

He found himself now altering that picture of the future. And with Louise in the picture, the altering wasn't difficult. A woman would change things, surely. He envisioned the house a little more solidly built than he might have done for himself. He'd expand the flower beds under the eaves to give it some extra colour. He wouldn't have to change the location. There wasn't a better site on the RS Connected for a main ranch house than the spot he'd selected and had been working.

But that was dreaming. This girl was too young to know what she wanted. He had a responsibility to her father's memory to see she got well-situated with a good young man who could care for her properly. And even if he and she did get together, there was plenty to do first. There was Big Jim, and there was Simon. There was no point in making any plans until those problems had been faced.

Near Rafferty's cabin, there was one ridge that came down out of the mountain mass, cutting into the valley floor. Rafferty knew a way over it, but now he took the easier trail that followed the base of the ridge and brought them around to within sight of the cabin. It was a good thing he had, since the trail took a rider to within calling distance of the place, and just now, that was no place to be.

Seven riders were fanned out below the cabin, facing Briggs and Rafferty. One of them, dressed in a fancy gambler's outfit, he figured to be Simon.

Rafferty pulled up.

'Louise, I'm going to make a diversion, and you run for it. I'll start riding and shooting over to our right. I figure that'll keep their attention on me, and give you a chance to get back in the protection of that ridge. Then you can make it to town.'

'Sorry, Hugh. I know you mean well, but I'm not going. We're facing this together. Maybe you didn't understand what I told you earlier, but I was serious. I'm a grown woman, and I can make up my own mind. I want you. I've seen how you look at me when you think I'm not looking. I think you want me, too. You can send me away, and I'll be gone for good. Is that what you want?'

'Well, no, of course not . . . .' Hugh sputtered. By the time it had occurred to him that he should have sent her away for her own safety, even if it meant losing her, it was too late.

'That's it, then. I accept.'

'What?'

'I accept your proposal. I'd like to be married up by the new house, but we can work on the details later. Let's handle this problem now.'

Rafferty knew he was whipped, and he grinned a silly grin of submission, shaking his head. Well, if he had to face this crowd, there weren't many people he'd have preferred to have with him.

Rafferty looked back at the gunmen ranged out before them, a quarter mile off. They could still run, but they were in open country, and it'd be a horse race. Maybe it was time to see this out. He stared at the figure in grey, Simon. The

148

man looked somehow familiar, but without a closer look, he couldn't be sure.

He heard a sound, and looked at Louise. She had her rifle out, pointed at the base of the treeline, a hundred yards to their left. A huge man in a long, dark coat rode out of the cover of the firs. Big Jim! Well, he was closer than the others, so he'd have to be dealt with first.

'If he wants it, we'll take it to him,' Rafferty said.

'He hasn't got a chance. I'm keeping him in my sights,' she said.

One of the gunmen up the hillside rode over to Simon, pointing at Big Jim and saying something. Simon nodded, and they kept their position. Rafferty guessed they'd let Jim do their work for them.

The big man rode up to Rafferty and Louise Briggs.

CHAPTER TWENTY-SIX

Big Jim Dunedin did not appear threatening. He rode with both hands on his reins, and he kept them high. His Sharps was in its scabbard, and he did not seem like a man given to cheap tricks like sleeve guns. Ten yards away, he stopped and raised his right hand, palm forward, in an ancient gesture of greeting and peace.

'Say your piece, Jim, and then we can do what needs doing,' Rafferty said.

'I'm not after you, Rafferty. I'm here to talk. But mebbe we'd better handle this little problem you got upslope before we do it,' the big man said.

'I don't know what you got in mind, but we surely can use the help,' Rafferty said.

'Yep. There's those seven up there, and then there's somebody been lurking around down in that copse of trees by the stream. There's a horse down there too, kind of grazing nearby and without any gear on him, but he's not wandering. I suspect he belongs to the man in the woods.'

Rafferty swung around, catching sight of the horse.

'Oh, hell, that's Baker.' He whistled and swung his arm.

The dark man stepped out of the trees and placed a bridle on the horse. He swung up bareback and rode to them, his rifle held in his right fist.

Rafferty grinned. 'You two been watching each other long?'

'I guess the last couple of hours we've been sort of stalking each other from across the grass. You two gonna save your fight for later?' Baker said.

'I got no fight with Rafferty,' Jim said. 'But it appears them boys up the hill might be getting a little restless, now that we evened up the odds some.'

'Let's take it to them,' Louise said. The black man and the mountain man just glanced at her, and turned their horses up the slope, riding wide enough apart that the gunmen wouldn't have a group target. Rafferty and Louise Briggs took up positions between the two and headed their horses toward the fight.

As they approached, Rafferty finally recognized Simon.

'The man in grey – Simon. His real name is Jack Katlin. I had a run-in with him once in the Rangers. He's a riverboat gambler. Has a cross-draw, and he's been known to wear a sleeve gun,' Rafferty said.

'The rest of these boys look like pretty straightforward gunhands,' Baker said. He still carried his rifle in his right hand, but now the barrel had lifted up some, and the butt rested on his hip. 'I'll take the two on the right, and then I'll try and help with the third one in.'

Big Jim chuckled. 'Why, I imagine two or three on the left are right in my sights.' Rafferty looked over to see Jim take his reins in his teeth. He had a gleaming new .45 Peacemaker Colt in each fist. Dunedin liked his guns. These were bigger than the pistols he'd carried when they'd last met, but they still looked like toys in those massive hands. He and his horse were clearly old friends, for the horse changed directions with the slightest push from Big Jim's knees.

'Well, shucks,' Rafferty said. 'That just leaves Katlin for me. You boys sure you don't want to take him, too?'

'You'd better handle him, Rafferty. Be bad for your reputation if you went into a gunfight and never fired a round. But if you need help, when I'm done with mine, I'll toss some lead his way,' Big Jim said.

'You all are forgetting the future Mrs Rafferty,' Louise said. 'Why don't you just let me have the men on both sides of Katlin?'

This would be no fast-draw gunfight. All four on Rafferty's side had their guns out, and several of Katlin–Simon's men had their own rifles pointed down the slope as the four approached. When they were within speaking distance, Rafferty called out.

'Jack Katlin! You been beaten at every turn. Why don't you give up and ride on out of here. It's not your kind of place, anyhow. You like a riverboat's lights and smoky gambling rooms.'

'So, finally you know me. Well, you're right, Rafferty. It's not my kind of place, but I can make it so. There's money to be made here. More money than you'll ever see. With it, I can go back to New Orleans and run the show. No more gambling for small stakes. I'll own a place, and buy one of the plantations, build a big Southern plantation mansion. This place will buy all that for me.'

'There's not enough grazing land to make it that way. I hear you been telling your boys about gold. Well, I've been all over this range, and there's not enough gold to buy up a few sections of Louisiana swamp land, much less good farm country. And as for that other story I heard from Kern, why, it just don't make sense.'

'Gold was the story I told the boys I sent after you, to keep them interested. It was just a cover story. I know there's no gold here, but you can get to the gold from here.

That's what you don't understand.'

'I guess I don't,' Rafferty said, letting him talk.

'With a little blasting powder, I can close the valley where it leads down to Springwater. I can make this a regular hole in the wall.'

'How are you going to get out, if you blast the only entrance.' Rafferty had heard the story from Kern, but he didn't tell Katlin that. He needed the time to think, and the man seemed to want to spill his scheme. After all, he had seven guns to four, and one of the four a woman. Katlin wouldn't know that Louise Briggs shot better than most men.

'That's the whole thing, Rafferty. It's not the only entrance, but it's the only one most people know about. There's an ancient trail back there. It takes a rider right up to the rim. From there, I've scouted three different trails that hook up to established trails. They all lead in different directions. Two of them catch stage routes and the other one gives access to a half dozen small towns.

'Those stages carry payrolls for the mines in this country, and they carry the profits from cattle sales. The towns have banks, and those banks are ripe for the picking. And after each job, the boys can come back here, down that hidden trail, and they'll never be found. In return for a place to hole up, they give me a piece of the action. For some of them, I'll plan the jobs and get a bigger cut. It's a foolproof plan.'

Quanah Baker spoke up.

'It might have been foolproof before, but it's a waste of time now. You remember two days ago that quake we had, the earth shaking? Well, I found that trail, and I was riding away from it when the earthquake hit. It caused a slide. A whole section of that mountain came down. It took the middle of that trail, wiped it out entirely, and dumped the rock and mud down on the lower section. Nobody's going up or down that route again, not ever,' Baker said, a queer sort of smile on his face.

Katlin grew red, the muscles tensing around his mouth.

'You lie!' he said, sort of jerking his shoulder and lifting his right hand to point at Baker.

CHAPTER TWENTY-SEVEN

Two shots erupted.

Katlin was thrown from the back of his horse before his men could react. A plume of smoke rose from Rafferty's pistol. Another puff hung in the air over Katlin's horse. Baker was holding his shoulder.

'It was his sleeve gun,' Rafferty said. 'That's how he got it out, by shaking his shoulder some to drop it into his hand, and then stretching out his arm. I saw it slipping into his fist, so I fired. He got a shot off, but I think I spoiled his aim.'

'Could have spoiled it a little more,' Baker said. 'That shot grazed me.'

Big Jim and Louise Briggs still had their guns on Katlin's men. Big Jim Dunedin spoke up, addressing Katlin's gunfighters.

'You boys still hot for a gunfight? You got no boss to fight for, and the reason for the fight is done. I were you, I'd slope on out of this valley and head for new territory. You, Kid Samuels, and you, Bill Rivers. I know you two. I know you're handy with guns. If you know me, you know I don't kill easy. I'd just as soon not see either of you, or any of these others, in this country again.'

The man identified as Rivers slowly lowered his rifle, making it clear his finger was nowhere near the trigger, and put it away. He lifted his hands, holding the reins high on his chest.

'I got no more fight here. Boys, this here's Big Jim Dunedin, the mountain man, an' if you ain't heard of Quanah Baker over there, you should know to leave him alone. Let's go someplace and get a drink,' Rivers said.

'Take Katlin's body with you. I don't want him on my range,' Rafferty said. Two of the men threw the corpse over his saddle. They tied him down and led him off, Katlin's horse the last in a single file heading down the hill toward the entrance to the ranch.

Katlin's gun lay in the grass. Dunedin stepped down out of the saddle and picked up the pearl-handled weapon.

'Remington double derringer,' he said. 'A new gun. Never seen one, but I heard it described. Even if you didn't spoil Katlin's aim, Rafferty, he still might've missed. A three-inch barrel don't carry a .41 calibre slug real straight.

'On the other hand, these new Colts of mine carry right nice. I came on a herd of antelope last month and decided to try them out. I fired them both at once, and got game with each shot. Fine weapon. 'Course, mebbe I was lucky.'

There was a dead tree fifteen yards away. He lifted the small twin-barrel pistol and fired the second chamber. A limb lifted off the side of the tree and dropped to the ground.

'I guess this thing shoots straighter than I thought. Could be useful at close quarters with grizzly. Anybody mind if I keep it?' Nobody minded.

CHAPTER TWENTY-EIGHT

Louise led the men up to the cabin. Wolf, lying on the porch, roused as they came up, and painfully managed to get up on all four legs.

'Look at that, Rafferty,' Louise said. 'He's getting better. Looks like his back legs are starting to work again.' Rafferty crouched and tousled the big dog's ruff. Louise went inside and got a fire started for coffee.

Big Jim Dunedin stood with his back to the cabin, looking out over the range. Rafferty got up and stood by him, speaking tentatively.

'You know I shot your brother,' Rafferty said to Big Jim Dunedin.

'I know you did, but I can't be taking after you for that. Rafferty, you gave me a chance and you gave that boy a chance. I tried my best with him, but he just had a wild hair that I couldn't tame.

'He ran into that man Simon or Katlin on the river. The gambler already knew about this place then. He paid Johnny a pile of money, with the promise of more if he killed you.

'I could have told him he wasn't good enough to take you, but he was off by himself, young and stupid, and he never asked, of course. Then when you shot him, Katlin got a message to me, saying you'd murdered Johnny and that there was money in it for me if I took care of you.

'Well, Rafferty. I don't take to killing for money and I don't take to people who pay for their killing. Seemed to me there was something strange here, so I did some checking around. When I found out where the truth was, I figured if I belonged on any side in this fight, it was yours.

'Somebody would have killed Johnny sometime, and I might have had to go after that man. But Johnny owed you, and I guess I owed you somehow, and it surely wasn't right that he should come after you. I can't blame you for that.'

Rafferty held out his hand, and the big man shook it.

'One thing,' Dunedin said. 'I want you to tell me how it was with you and Johnny. The family will want to know.'

Rafferty turned to face Big Jim.

'He was a man, Jim. I can say that. There was no yellow in him. He had to know I was good, but he came right up to me. He said, "Rafferty, I took good money to kill you, and I got to do it." I told him, "Boy, you can try." '

'We were up near where that mountain trail must be. I had some cows back there I was chasing out of the brush. I needed to get the bad stock out, because I want to develop a good breed of cow on the RS Connected. Finally, I did a bloody hide roundup. You know. I shot one, and hung its hide on a tree. Those cows are plain curious, and they just come out and gathered around the smell of that hide. I was up above them, and I came down and just kind of pushed them into the main valley.'

'Works the same way with buffalo,' Dunedin said. 'I never liked it much, but some of the old timers, they'd shoot an old cow through the lungs, so she'd still stand, but she'd bleed. The other buffalo would just mill round at the smell of it, and you could pick them off easy.'

'Same idea. Well, I was making a lot of noise, driving

those cows of mine down to the valley, where I'd rigged me up a corral with dried brush and branches, so I could separate them. Johnny was on his horse and he came out of a little gully where he had a camp. He rode right up and talked to me, and then he drew.

'He had the drop on me, but his gun misfired. By the time he got the second shot off, I had lead in him. He died quick, and I buried him up there. I have his gun back here in a rag. You can have it.'

Rafferty stepped into the cabin and brought it out. Dunedin inspected the worn weapon.

'Used to be mine,' Big Jim said. 'Old, worn out Walker Colt. Generally a good gun, but this one's got a curse on it, I guess. I took it off a dead man, an' mebbe it failed him, too. It was beat up then, and rusty, but I fixed it up and used it a few years, and then I gave it to the boy. Rafferty, I don't want this gun. You can keep it.'

Rafferty wrapped it up and put it back on the shelf.

'I'm sorry about the boy, and I appreciate your backing me here, Jim,' he said.

'He had it coming, I guess. I'm glad it was clean and fast. Mebbe there's a certain rightness in it, that a man's gun should fail when he's taken money for a killing. God knows it don't happen enough. Like I said, I don't hold it against you,' Dunedin said. 'I've said what I needed to say. I'll be heading out now.'

'I want you to know that if you ever have trouble, you've got a place to come here on the RS. And if you're passing through, you're always welcome,' Rafferty said.

'More than that,' Louise said. 'I want you to count on coming back here in five or six years. I expect to have a few young Raffertys running around then, and they'll need an uncle who can teach them some mountain skills.'

The big man, pulling on his long, black coat, nodded. 'I appreciate that, ma'am. I do. But this is the range where my

159

only brother died. And as much as I don't blame Rafferty here, losing Johnny is going to gnaw on me for a long time. I don't think I'll be back in this country.'

He mounted and rode off, but cut up the valley.

'Where's he going?' Rafferty said, turning to Baker.

'Probably going to find the boy's grave, say a few words. And then probably going up the old trail,' the black man replied.

'You said it was destroyed in the quake.'

'I said that, but it wasn't true. Big Jim knew about that trail all along. He came into the valley that way. I trailed him. And he was up in those parts yesterday, after the quake. That trail is as old as these hills. It'll take more than a little temblor to take it down. Big Jim knew it was still there.'

'What about you, Quanah?'

'Me, well, I guess there's some work to be done on this ranch, a house to build. I figure to stay around to the wedding, anyhow.'

Louise spoke.

'You'd better, Quanah Baker. Somebody's got to stand up for me, and it looks like you're going to have to be it. It'd make my dad proud.'

'Make me proud, too, Louise. Thanks. And afterwards, I might head out and try and find myself my own little range. We're none of us getting any younger.'

Rafferty crouched down and scratched a crude map into the earth.

'You know, Quanah? I have a place in mind, and unless I'm mistaken, it shouldn't be far from the top of the trail Big Jim's taking. Maybe tomorrow we should ride that trail and look it over.'